# THE CURSED PORTRAIT

## A REGENCY PARANORMAL ROMANCE

ELLIE ST. CLAIR

♥ **Copyright 2024 Ellie St Clair**

**All rights reserved.**

This book or parts thereof may not be reproduced in any form, stored in any retrieval system, or transmitted in any form by any means—electronic, mechanical, photocopy, recording, or otherwise—without prior written permission of the publisher.

Facebook: Ellie St. Clair

Cover by AJF Designs

Do you love historical romance? Receive access to a free ebook, as well as exclusive content such as giveaways, contests, freebies and advance notice of pre-orders through my mailing list!

Sign up here!

**Also By Ellie St. Clair**

*Standalone*

The Cursed Portrait
Always Your Love
The Stormswept Stowaway
A Touch of Temptation

Regency Summer Nights Box Set
Regency Romance Series Starter Box Set

For a full list of all of Ellie's books, please see
www.elliestclair.com/books.

# CHAPTER 1

*A*melia's fingertips tingled as she stepped out of the carriage.

She fisted them into her hands to soothe their unease while she swiveled her head from side to side, expecting a presence lurking in the shadows.

All she saw was a line of carriages extending down the drive.

It seemed she was not the only one interested in the mysterious Blackwood art collection.

Although knowing London society, it was not the collection most of them were interested in, but rather the owner of it all. The Earl of Blackwood – as much of an enigma as the house and the display itself.

Amelia reached into the hidden pocket of her dress, running her fingers over the smooth parchment that had arrived at her door two weeks ago, inviting her to the art exhibition ball.

She had a feeling that she had not been invited for her social status.

Her lips curled into a smile as she ascended the steps of

the great house, which stood on the rise overlooking all of Hamstead. The earl was so rarely seen in the city that Amelia guessed he appreciated his family's London home was a good six miles from the heart of London.

Not that any of it mattered to Amelia.

She was here for another purpose entirely.

She had much to pay for – the carriage ride here, the toll she'd had to pay at the Spaniard's Inn to cross into Hampton, and most importantly, the crimson gown she had purchased specifically for this evening. It had better all be worth it.

"Good evening," the butler greeted her as he took her cloak. The slight widening of his eyes was the only suggestion that her dress might not be what was expected at such a gathering.

She had not, however, intended to fit in.

"Good evening," she responded, her gaze already drifting around the foyer, noting the light from the candles notched into the chandelier, dancing over the room as it reflected off of the elaborate formation of crystals.

Her slippers slid over the polished marble beneath her feet, and while this was all designed for opulence, she couldn't help but note that the gilded accents of the room's paneling were chipped, the paint of the pale pink walls faded, and the carpet up the sweeping staircase was worn with footsteps.

Perhaps there was a reason the earl was holding this surprising art exhibition.

"Amelia Lennox, is that you?"

A smile burst onto Amelia's face as she turned toward the voice behind her.

Charlie Bastian had just walked through the door, curling his mustache as he stepped toward her and enveloped her in a warm embrace that met with the disapproval of the couple who had walked in behind him, their noses upturned at such a display.

Amelia only prolonged the hold and smiled wickedly at them.

The woman gasped, and Amelia grinned even harder. It served her right.

Finally, Charlie released her and held her before him, his hands on her shoulders.

"Am I glad to see you! It's been weeks!"

"I know, far too long," she agreed. Charlie always lifted her spirits, and she should have sought him out earlier.

"You missed our last meeting," he said, his tone both hurt and accusatory at the same time.

"I know, Charlie. I am sorry for that," she said. "I had a job to finish."

If only that were true. In actuality, it was becoming increasingly difficult for her to hide her truth when she met with the conventional artists.

She didn't fit there – nor did she fit entirely at her other meetings, for she took as much pride in the creative aspects of her work as she did in the elemental.

"Well, do come next time, all right? You provide beauty there – and I am not just talking about your artwork."

When he winked, she jokingly rolled her eyes and took the arm he offered her, allowing him to lead her into the front parlor and through what was proving to be one of the most eclectic group of people she had ever seen together in one room – and that was saying a lot.

"What do you think we're doing here?" she asked as they were handed cups of what she realized, upon her first sip, was one of the finest wines she had ever tasted.

"My invitation said it was an art exhibition," Charlie murmured, looking around them and waving to another of their acquaintances who stood across the room in front of one of the high sash windows. "However, you would think that an earl's art exhibition would draw fellow nobles and patrons – not artists themselves."

"Only those of us well known for our talents are present."

"Nothing but the best for an earl," Charlie quipped.

"Do you think he is interested in adding to his collection?" she asked, her heartbeat increasing. She could only hope that was the case. A commission from an earl would go a long way in covering her expenses – most notably, her accommodations. She had no wish to move from Soho.

If she didn't have a commission soon, she would have to return to her less... savory methods of making money.

Although it was nothing she hadn't done before.

Her gaze roved around the room in search of the earl. She knew him only by reputation, and yet, she had a feeling that she would know him when she saw him. A man with such a collection as that in front of her – statues, paintings, and tapestries, most strategically aligned above the paneling or placed in front of the pale blue walls – would likely have a commanding air about him.

She had heard he was formidable, yet wondered what secrets he might hide.

Secrets she could learn and use for her own gain if she must, even though the thought of doing so already caused her stomach to churn.

She would have a lot of compensation to do to make up for it. Perhaps she could paint him something that would ease the loss.

Even if he didn't hire her tonight, she had options.

Charlie appeared to read her mind – although, thankfully, not the whole of it – as he leaned in. "I must leave you for a moment to speak to Mr. and Mrs. Anderson. I've heard they are looking for an artist to paint their entire family."

"This is quite the opportunity to meet and connect with patrons, is it not?" she murmured.

"Yes," he said with a wink. "I best go before you beat me to it and convince Mr. Anderson to hire you with that wicked gown of yours."

Amelia scoffed as she watched him go. He was talented, yes, but let him have the family portraits. She far preferred commissions that gave her more freedom than capturing the likeness of the person paying for the commission.

That never ended well, as, in her experience, the subjects often saw themselves in a much different light than they appeared.

Even if the artist could influence their emotions.

She should likely take Charlie's advice and meet potential patrons, but her feet seemed to have their own mind as she wandered out of the central area and toward the back of the house. The gallery had been set up in what she guessed was usually a parlor, while music emanated from a back room that was more likely a ballroom.

Amelia, however, had no time or interest in dancing.

Instead, she was drawn to explore the dark corners at the back of the house. She pushed open a door that was only slightly ajar, entering what appeared to be a study, one that immediately wrapped her in its quiet elegance and intellectual sophistication.

Rich, dark wood paneling lined the walls, creating a sense of warmth. The polished hardwood appeared to have been covered by a rug in the past, judging by the darker square on the floor beneath her. An imposing mahogany desk, its legs covered with intricate carvings and its polished surface with a quill, inkstand, and elegantly bound journal, was one of the only pieces of furniture in the room, the high-backed leather chair behind it and the floor-to-ceiling bookshelves, the others.

The heavy velvet drapes were closed while one oil lamp burned in its sconce on the wall, casting a flickering glow over the easel sitting in the center of the room.

Even if it hadn't been so prominently featured, Amelia would have been drawn to it.

Any person would have noted the beauty of the woman within it, dressed in rich, striking attire that Amelia would guess was from half a century ago, although she was no expert in fashions.

An art enthusiast would have commented on the portrait's damage, the cracks in the paint, the areas where the colors had faded.

Any artist would have noted the realistic style of the painting, with its intricate details and rich colors. The brushwork was masterful, capturing the light to give the portrait almost a lifelike quality.

But only Amelia would sense the painting's subtle, ethereal aura. The redheaded woman's serene expression on the surface held the emotion of the entire painting, the undercurrent of sadness or anger hinting at the turmoil she had experienced.

If Amelia was correct with her guess, that was.

She should not have been in the private study and was aware that this painting had likely been omitted from the gallery for a reason, but she couldn't pull herself away.

As she moved from side to side, the woman's eyes seemed to follow her, and Amelia leaned in as the painting drew her closer. "Who are you?" she whispered, expecting her question to be rhetorical.

Which was why she jumped nearly a foot in the air when she received a response.

* * *

# THE CURSED PORTRAIT

Lord Maximillian Waverly, the Earl of Blackwood, moved through his guests with more ease than he felt.

He supposed that was because they allowed him through – not because he was doing so out of his own choice.

No, if he had his way, he would not be here tonight, and none of these people would have stepped foot in his house to ogle his priceless pieces of artwork.

But his artwork was all that stood between him and ruin, so here they were. Patrons to admire his work and, hopefully, make him offers that he could discreetly accept without putting any of his pieces on sale or up for auction.

To do so would only advertise the fact that he had nothing left.

And he preferred to keep his family's secrets just that – secret.

No one needed to know the lengths he had to go to cover up the family's debts.

For every investment, every hand of cards – hell, every plot of land – had come to absolutely nothing over the past thirty years.

All of the wealth his family had once held was gone, the former opulence crumbling.

The only properties left were this London house and the Blackwood Estate, where he preferred to spend most of his time. The servants were kept to a minimum, and the furnishings were worn and bare.

Then his second purpose for this evening – to find an artist worthy enough to restore the painting he hoped to be rid of. A painting that could become fine enough in its richness to fetch a reasonable price and, hopefully, rid him of the curse that had plagued his family ever since it had been cast all those years ago.

He damned the woman in the portrait. He damned the

love that had led to the falling out. He damned the father who had caused such pain.

It had left him with absolutely nothing but the wreckage and the responsibility to right it all.

He had no choice.

And all of these family secrets? They would die with him. He would make certain of it.

"Lord Blackwood, there you are!"

He turned, forcing a smile onto his face as one of his mother's closest friends wrapped her hand around his arm.

"Lady Grantham, how are you?"

"Very well," she said, her eyes running over him as though assessing his health. "We had to attend when we received your invitation, although I must say, I was shocked that you would have all of these priceless pieces of art on display."

"Why should I be the only one to enjoy them?" he asked, raising a brow, hoping that would quell her curiosity, but apparently not.

"What would your mother think of this?" she said before leaning in slightly and lowering her voice. "There are all kinds of people here."

"I know," he said, leaning down conspiratorially. "I invited them."

He smiled at her shock of outrage, having to contain his chuckle.

She looked behind her as her husband walked up, as unfazed as ever.

"Lord Blackwood," he greeted Max, who returned his nod. "You have some lovely pieces here. Are they for sale?"

"No," Max said, which of course only caused interest to rise in the couple's faces. Exactly what he was hoping for. "If you will excuse me, I must see to a pressing matter. Please enjoy yourselves."

Gripping a glass of the last cask of wine from the cellar in his hand, he left the parlor, passing by the ballroom where society was amusing themselves on finally seeing behind the curtain he had cast over his house and his life.

Let them look. What did he care anymore?

He needed a reprieve, if only for a moment. He wished he could find his bedchamber, but then he would need to climb the front staircase where he might be seen. Instead, he would have to take refuge in the study – even if it meant sharing it with *her*.

He pushed through the door, expecting to be greeted by the seagreen eyes that had haunted him for the past twenty years.

But those were not the eyes that greeted him.

No, these belonged to another woman.

One who was just as captivating.

And, he felt deep within his soul, just as dangerous.

## CHAPTER 2

Amelia couldn't have said how long she had stood in the middle of the study, staring at the portrait.

Paintings had spoken to her in the past, sure. But never quite so literally.

She had just opened her mouth, finally ready to formulate a response to Miss Isolde, when the door swung open behind her, interrupting the conversation, as it was.

She stood still, shocked for a second time that evening, at the man standing at the entrance.

This was the Earl of Blackwood.

She would know him anywhere – even if he hadn't been entering his study.

Was she going to face repercussions for entering his private sanctum?

He shocked her – again – when he spoke, approaching her with slow, measured footsteps.

"You have happened upon one of the more... intriguing pieces in our collection," he said as though he had been expecting her here. "It has a certain allure, does it not?"

Did he know that the painting had called her to it? Amelia

finally recovered herself, forcing a smile in response, reminding herself that she needed this man – his money.

And that she shouldn't be as drawn to him as she had been to the painting.

"Indeed, it does. The brushwork is exquisite."

He nodded slowly, and Amelia sensed that she was being measured. Tested.

"What else do you see?" he asked, his voice low, velvety, as though he wished to lull her into sleep.

"Besides its condition?" she asked, raising a brow, and he nodded. Sensing what he wanted from her, she told the truth.

"It's holding secrets," she said, meeting his gaze brazenly. "The woman is tortured, and her emotion has extended to the rest of the painting. The brushwork's realism has captured her so that viewers *feel* her emotion in their very souls. Elements in the painting tell a story. The locket she wears is exquisite and holds meaning to her. The setting is where her heartbreak occurred. The objects on the table beside her are her personal effects, each of which signifies importance in her life."

She sensed rather than heard or saw the sharp intake of his breath, but he only nodded.

"You are perceptive," he noted. "And passionate about your work."

"You know who I am?" she asked.

"I invited you here," he said, leaning one hip against his desk. "You are Amelia Lennox, one of the few women who anyone of means will hire."

"You are too kind, my lord," she said, tilting her head to the side as she studied him the same way she did a piece of captivating artwork.

Long locks of dark hair extended over his forehead, covering a scar that cut through his eyebrow. His nose slightly bent more than would make him classically handsome, and he had a small dent in the chin amid a strong jawline.

Beyond the obvious, however, mystery was lurking in his gaze, more to him than he likely allowed others to see.

"Tell me, why *have* you invited me here?" she asked, not wanting to waste any more time.

He chuckled. "You are not at all like the young ladies I am used to."

"I would be highly suspicious if you said I was."

"Allow me to introduce myself. I am the Earl of Blackwood."

"I know. And you already know my name, so let us dispense with the pleasantries, shall we?"

"Very well," he said, amusement dancing across his face. "I invited you – as well as other artists of your ilk – to tonight's exhibition because I am interested in having this very painting restored."

"You could have hired one of us without all of the theatrics," she said, sensing more at play.

He fixed his dark stare upon her. "I had a dual purpose."

She wasn't going to get any more out of him.

"It needs much work," she said, turning to study it again, shaking off the shivers that touched her spine, unsure if they were caused by the painting or the man. "It has not been well cared for."

"It didn't deserve to be," he muttered.

"You did not care for Isolde?" she asked, arching a brow, surprised when he looked at her so sharply that the intensity of his gaze seemed to burn right through her.

"How do you know that name?" he demanded.

"I couldn't say," she said truthfully, for he would never believe her if she admitted it. "I just do."

His gaze turned dark and stormy as he fixed his eyes on

the painting behind her, almost as if he were admonishing the subject.

Perhaps he would have believed her after all, but she was not about to admit to her lie now. Once one started down a path, it was best not to retrace any steps, she had learned from experience.

"Have you seen my work?" she asked, attempting to change the subject before he continued on the matter.

"I have," he said. "My man-of-business provided me samples from those he considered the best in London."

"How flattering," she said. "Are you looking for a complete restoration?"

"I am."

"Do you have a timeline in mind?"

"A few months would be ideal," he said.

"I could start in a week," she said, before realizing she likely seemed far too eager. "You are fortunate for I have a rare break in commissions."

"I do not believe I have yet offered the job," he said, arching an eyebrow, the slight scar that ran through it becoming more prominent when he did.

She shrugged. "I am the best. You should secure me quickly."

"There is a stipulation," he said. "The work will be done at Blackwood Manor."

Another surprise. For a woman who was very rarely surprised. "Outside of London? You do not trust me with the painting, then."

"That is part of it," he admitted. "I have other reasons for not wanting the painting outside of my possession. Reasons I am not inclined to share. This is the first time it has left Blackwood Manor since its creation."

"I see," she murmured, already running the numbers in her

head. She loved Soho, but she had no ties to her current residence. Not only could she likely make a generous amount from what would be a straightforward and yet intriguing job, but she wouldn't have to pay for accommodations for a few months, at least. Longer, if she could stretch it out. And an earl could make for a good future client. "That could be arranged."

"Very good. My man-of-business will be in touch." He held out his elbow toward her. "Shall we return to the party? I will show you around the rest of my gallery if you're interested."

"I would be very interested." She couldn't wait for Charlie to see her up close with the earl, imagining his expression when he realized she had captured the commission they had all desperately longed for.

She smiled up at the earl as she slipped her arm through his, the bare skin of her wrist brushing against his hand as she did.

Causing an eruption.

Her smile fell, her entire body going slack as power gushed from where they touched, racing through her and filling her from head to toe until she thought she might explode from the vibrations.

The last thing she saw were his eyes, staring at her with equal shock and confusion.

Then everything went black.

\* \* \*

*Now you've done it.*

"Shut up!" Max yelled at the voices inside his head, voices that were going to drive him mad if he wasn't already there. He ignored them as he lifted the woman in his arms, carrying her over to the desk. Holding her steady with his hip, he

THE CURSED PORTRAIT

cleared the surface with one swoop of his arm and then placed her on top of it.

This was why people had furniture.

Isolde's eyes were judging him as he shook Miss Lennox by her shoulders gently yet firmly, willing her awake.

Even while, inside, he was shaking as much as she had been.

His body was more alive than ever before, tingling as the earth beneath him threatened to swallow him whole, the tips of his fingers burning.

Who the hell was this woman?

None of the research he had been provided suggested that she was anything more than an artist, and yet – and yet.

*There is one way to wake a woman.*

He ignored the voice that had taken up residence in his head months ago as he felt for her pulse, relieved when he found it beating strongly beneath his fingers.

Thank goodness.

That wouldn't have been easy to explain – not that the only reason he wanted her alive was so that he wouldn't be accused of murder.

He needed her to restore the painting.

*And she is more alluring than any woman you've ever met.*

True. He could admit that. Not that he would ever act upon such an inkling.

*Touch her.*

He frowned at the painting. The last thing he needed was Isolde's interference.

*You have no better ideas.*

This voice was the usual one, the man who had pushed his way into his thoughts, following him around, giving him no reprieve no matter where he was.

"Very well," he muttered, giving in and reaching out, cupping Miss Lennox's face in his hands, trying to ignore how the soft creaminess of her skin was begging for more than just his fingers upon it. His lips would do nicely.

He pushed away the thought as he leaned in and cupped her face, prepared this time for the jolt that ran through him.

Water. He needed water. He looked around the room for a cup of it, but there was none to be found – even his costly glass of wine had fallen to the floor when he had cleared the desk to lay her upon it, and he stocked no sideboard here.

When he turned his attention back to the prostrate woman, however, he was astonished to find that tears were leaking out of her eyes as though he had summoned them himself. He brushed them over her face, hoping that, in some way, they would revive her.

When his thumbs stroked her lips she gasped and jolted upward so quickly that he had to snap his head back to prevent the two of them from smashing their noses against one another.

"Who are you?" she demanded instantly, her eyes narrowing, and he gritted his teeth to prevent himself from snapping back to her demand.

"I am the Earl of Blackwood, as you well know," he said, his voice clipped. "And I would watch my tone if I were you."

Her brows rose and she opened her mouth as though to retort, but she finally caught herself, looking around them before back at him.

She closed her mouth and pushed him away as she scooted toward the end of the table, ignoring the hand of assistance he offered.

"What did you do to me?" she asked now, to which he snorted, no longer quite so concerned about her. She hadn't stricken him as a woman who would have fainted upon the touch of an earl, but then, one could never know another's true intentions for certain.

"Besides grace you with my presence?" he asked, giving her the cause to snort this time.

"Sure. We shall go with that."

"Absolutely nothing," he said. "I offered you my arm and you were overcome."

"I was—" her mouth snapped shut again, although her eyes told another story, storms brewing within them. "Very well. I am going to return to the party."

"I will accompany you."

"No," she said firmly. "I believe I will go alone."

She strode to the door, about to open it when he called out, "Miss Lennox?"

"Yes?" she said without turning around.

"Would you still like that commission?"

"I would," she said with one quick look behind her, meeting his eyes before her gaze continued on to the painting. "*She* can't hurt me."

As she shut the door behind her, Max shook his head.

If only she knew how wrong she was.

He could have sworn that Isolde was laughing in agreement.

# CHAPTER 3

"You cannot go there alone."

Amelia sighed, knowing that Charlie had a point, but what was she supposed to do?

After the party, a night in which she hadn't seen the earl again after their encounter in the study, she had received a message inviting her to his country home along with his offer for the restoration of the painting – one that was far too generous to even consider turning down.

"Charlie, there are likely more servants living at Blackwood Manor than there are people in the entirety of my building."

She motioned to the room around her, one which Charlie was going to inhabit while she was gone. He had been interested in moving into this building for months now, although she hadn't been certain whether it was her or the accommodations that enticed him.

"I should come with you."

"You are more than welcome to, but the earl is not going to pay you for any further work. He seems intent upon this painting and this painting alone."

"His pieces at the exhibition would be worth a fortune. Why does he care so much about this one?"

"That," she said, grunting as she tugged her heavy valise out the door, "is what I shall soon find out."

"Will he be in residence?"

She paused, realizing that she had assumed he would be in the country with her, and distressingly finding herself perturbed by the suggestion that he might not. "I am not actually sure," she said. "He offered me the job at the party, and then I received a note the next day formally hiring me."

"Have you ever seen Blackwood Manor?"

"Of course not."

"It is in Norfolk. That is a rather far distance to travel."

"Why? Are you planning to visit me, Charlie?"

"What if I was?" His question caused the air between them to suddenly fill with uncomfortable tension, and Amelia realized with a sinking heart that this man, who she considered one of her very best friends, might have an inkling there actually could be more between them.

She had suspected it for a time but had convinced herself that she was reading too much into it, that it was just surface level.

She had always wanted to share her life with another and could be called a romantic, even if she showed no outward sign of having such an affliction or had any urge to settle. She didn't have to – she did just fine on her own.

But she didn't feel that way toward Charlie. She wished she did, for he made her laugh and was always such a vibrant presence in her life, but when they touched, there was no spark there.

This reminded her of her circumstances with the earl – a spark that had ignited.

She shook off the thought as she leaned over and placed a hand on Charlie's arm. He was still one of her closest friends.

"I have something for you," she said, walking over to the armoire in the corner, finding the few pieces of charcoal she had left behind along with a piece of parchment. She had considered that Charlie was likely to use them, and she had included the supplies on the list she had sent back to the earl for purchase.

She took the charcoal in her hand and, closing her eyes, envisioned another woman, one who would be perfect for Charlie. She hoped that she was creating someone who could make him happy. She placed all of her wishes for him into the drawing as he silently watched her before she lifted it and held it outward to him.

"For you."

He looked down in awe.

"You drew that so quickly."

"It's just a sketch," she said with a slightly embarrassed shrug. "I'll make you another. With color next time."

"No need," he said, his throat seemingly clogged with emotion. "It's.... more than enough. Who is it?"

She beamed, happy that she had been able to spread the hope and joy that she had been meaning to. "I thought of what happiness would mean to you and that emerged."

"Let me walk you to the coach?"

"The earl has sent a carriage for me."

"How fancy," he said, ire in his tone.

"Tell me, Charlie," she said, changing the subject. "Did you receive the commission from the Andersons that you were chasing at the party?"

"I did, actually," he said, cheery once more. "I start right away."

"I'm so glad." She leaned in once they reached the bottom of the stairs. "Will you still allow a kiss on the cheek?" He turned his cheek to her before she quickly pressed her lips upon it and then leaned in toward him and squeezed. "I do love you, Charlie. Be good while I'm gone. You're such a good friend."

"Don't be too long, you hear?" he said as the carriage rolled up in front of them, and Amelia blinked at its grandeur. As an artist, the nobility usually appreciated her skills, and yet that didn't mean they would consider her value significant enough to send such a carriage for her.

"Write to me when you arrive," Charlie called out as the coach's driver hefted her valise onto the boot and she climbed in, running her hand over the velvet cushions beneath her.

"I will," she said, waving out the window. "I promise."

And with that, the coach rolled away, soon leaving London behind.

\* \* \*

MAX SHOULDN'T BE HERE.

He should have remained in Hampstead while the woman was in the manor, working with the cursed painting.

It would have been far better that way, especially after what had happened the last time they had touched.

But he didn't seem to have it within him to stay away.

At least he hadn't insisted they ride to Blackwood Manor together, although he had made sure that his carriage would see her safely there. He couldn't stand the thought of her crammed into a stagecoach for hours on end, even if her comfort should have no bearing on him whatsoever, so long as she was able to perform her duties.

He had set the painting in what had been, at one time, the music room, although no one alive had used it for years now.

He had been told *she* had loved it. Isolde. Which made it fitting that this was where she would find new life.

"Enjoy this," he said to the painting as he walked out of the door. "For it will be the last you will see of this house."

He tripped over apparently nothing as he crossed the threshold, and he cursed as he shivered. "Damn ghosts," he muttered.

"My lord," came a voice – a human one, thank goodness – from the adjacent drawing room. "I hear we are to have a visitor."

"We are. An artist who will be seeing to the restoration of the portrait."

"I see," said the ever-stoic Whitaker. "It will be good to have company. Will she be eating with you or with us downstairs?"

Max paused. She was performing a service for him, like anyone else in the household. A comfortable guest bedroom would be fitting, although perhaps not in his wing. And yet.... He met the butler's inquisitive stare, his response formulating itself.

"With me," he said, that fiery feeling washing over him once more. The moment he had laid eyes on her, he had known that she belonged with him – as an artist, of course, restoring the painting.

Nothing more.

No one could ever mean anything more to him. This curse was dying with him, he reminded himself. No love story had ever ended well in his family. No life, for that matter, not since the curse had been set. Chances were that he wouldn't make it to the following year, let alone long enough to sire any children.

But he could enjoy some company for a while, could he not?

*You should tell her.*

That certainly wasn't the butler's voice. Max inwardly

sighed, as he had hoped the voices had silenced themselves for a time, but it seemed they had returned.

*There is nothing to tell,* he thought back, although to whom, he had no idea.

*Together, you were so powerful she lost consciousness. Think what you could do. What you could be.*

"Nonsense," he said out loud, so forcefully that the normally nonplussed butler, who had begun to walk away, jumped across the foyer.

"Apologies, Whitaker," he said grimly. "I just… tripped."

Not a lie.

He wasn't going to have to worry about keeping himself away from this woman once she arrived.

For a short bit of time with him would likely have her running away.

\* \* \*

AMELIA DIDN'T HAVE to look out the carriage window to know that they were nearing Blackwood Manor. There was a change in the air, one that the impending nightfall couldn't explain.

It was cooler here. The air was filled with a muted silence and oppression had fallen over them like a protective shield.

She pushed herself off the seat, leaning out the window as the woodland moved by her, craning her neck to see the house itself better.

The sprawling manor had obviously sat here for decades, if not centuries, its opulence at once both terrifying and amazing. Yet, somewhere beneath it was an underlying gloom, the same that she had sensed within the earl as well as the painting itself.

Interesting.

She was still staring up at the grand estate when the carriage pulled to a stop at the end of the long, winding gravel road, which was lined with ancient trees and empty, decorative lanterns. Here at the end of the driveway, the tall wrought-iron gates with intricate designs marked the entrance, flanked by stone pillars topped with statues of heraldic animals.

The manor's light-colored stone gave it a timeless appearance. Amelia walked under the grand portico of the front entrance, which was supported by tall Corinthian columns. Empty urns lined the broad stone steps, these flanked by untrimmed topiary that gave a rather menacing look to what had likely been a welcoming entrance at one point in time.

It had obviously been built to exude history and timelessness, but there was more here.

There was magic beyond it all. Had it always been this way?

"Miss Lennox, how wonderful to have you with us," said an overly cheerful butler as he opened the door to her, surprising her. Amelia would have guessed that a butler of such a manor would be a hulking giant of a man, lurking in his motions and as grim in the face as the vegetation beyond.

"Thank you," she said with equal cheerfulness. "I am happy to be here."

An additional three servants greeted her, each with such interest that she wondered whether they had seen anyone besides one another in a time.

The housekeeper was warm as she led her up the stairs to what would be her bedroom for her stay.

"I am surprised that I am staying in a guest room, actually," Amelia said. "I would have been happy in the servants' quarters."

"It's good for the earl to have company," the housekeeper, Mrs. Bloom, said. "He has been so lonely. Ever since—"

She stopped, sensing she was saying too much, although Amelia silently urged her on. She wished she had her paints in her hands and not in her bag so that she could physically ask her for more. She knew better than to push at the moment, however.

"I would be happy to be some company for him, although I am here to restore a painting."

"Oh yes," Mrs. Bloom said, her smile now strained as she pulled a ring of keys from her pocket and opened the bedroom doors, slightly disconcerting to Amelia as she wondered why a bedroom might need to be locked in a manor consisting only of an earl and his servants. "The painting."

"Where is it?" Amelia asked as she pushed through and took in what would be her home for the next few months. The bedroom, which had likely been grand at one point in time, was showing signs of neglect. The faded floral wallpaper was peeling at the edges, while the slightly sagging four-poster bed was draped in threadbare light blue velvet curtains. A few pieces of mahogany furniture sat by the fireplace while the worn rug underfoot bore the marks of age.

"In the music room, I'm told," the housekeeper said. "It is a pretty room. There are many windows overlooking the back garden."

"Lovely," Amelia murmured, sensing more to the story but knowing that this was not the time nor the person to ask.

"It is rather late," Mrs. Bloom said. "Would you like help unpacking?"

"No, thank you," Amelia said. "I am accustomed to taking care of myself."

And she didn't want anyone else touching her supplies.

"Very good. If you'd like dinner, we could bring it here."

"Perhaps I will take it in the music room if you don't mind," Amelia said. She had no intentions of touching the painting with food close by, but she would prefer to sit with it for a time before actually taking a brush to it.

It was time to speak to Isolde again.

## CHAPTER 4

*She* was here.

Max sensed Miss Lennox's presence in the manor before anyone even alerted him to her arrival – which was disconcerting, to say the least. No woman had ever had this hold on him before – especially one he had only just met.

"My lord?"

"I know," Max responded to Whitaker from where he was bent over his ledgers in the study, the fire crackling in the hearth beyond.

He had been working diligently to ensure that all was put to rights before his time came—whenever that might be. If his ancestors' age of passing before him were any indication, it would be soon.

Unfortunately, no matter how creatively he added the numbers, they all amounted to the same. Less than nothing.

Max opened the page of the ledger detailing each piece of artwork in his collection, which was a considerably long list. He had only brought a small selection to Hampstead.

So far, he had received letters of offer for three of the statues and two of the paintings, which had been exactly what he had been hoping for – patrons who would express interest even if he hadn't noted that the items were for sale. Most of the potential buyers likely wanted them for that exact reason, for it was far more fun to think that they were stealing something away from him.

He snorted. The chance of all of this falling through was high. He should tamp down any hope that might arise.

Hope was the last thing that a man like him needed in his life.

"Mrs. Bloom showed Miss Lennox to her chamber, but she soon made her way to the music room," Whitaker said. "She wanted to spend time with the portrait." He visibly shuddered before walking away.

This was the very reason he had hired her. He had never before met someone who was actually drawn to the portrait of Isolde – everyone else ran from it as though it was chasing them.

Which, he supposed, in a way, it was.

While Miss Lennox had obviously felt that the portrait expressed emotions, she had accepted it for what it was.

He realized that he had read over the ledger about five separate times, the words still dancing across the page in front of him. Ever since Miss Lennox had stepped foot in the house, he hadn't been able to concentrate. It was as though he was being pulled toward her, out of his seat and to the music room, his feet knowing the way even if Whitaker hadn't told him just where he would have been able to find her.

He slammed the book shut.

It seemed his work was finished for tonight.

* * *

AMELIA IGNORED the tray sitting beside her, as tantalizing as the scent of perfectly cooked beef with the side of roasted potatoes was.

Since she had entered the music room, she had been just as captivated by the portrait as she had been the first time she had laid eyes on it.

Only now, it was as though she was being welcomed home by Isolde herself.

"Good evening," she said cautiously, taking a seat in front of it. "Since we are going to be spending a great deal of time together, I thought it was best we get to know one another."

She stared at the portrait, and while Isolde stared right back, this time she did not say a word.

At least, not that Amelia could hear.

"Nothing, then? I am not here to hurt you, if that is your concern."

Amelia tilted her head, studying the crimson curtains behind Isolde, as well as the items on the table and the locket around her neck.

"Whoever commissioned this painting wanted to remember your true self," she murmured, her eyes widening with the discovery. She could be wrong. But most portraits from past eras showed perfectly posed subjects with the most formal of garments and stuffy of backgrounds. Not this one.

"Why the melancholy?" she wondered aloud, standing and walking back and forth in front of the painting, tapping her index finger against her lips. "What happened to cause such sorrow, if someone loved you enough to have you painted in your vivacity? And then why were you shut away to cause this much destruction to the painting?"

Isolde stared back as though willing Amelia to figure this out for herself.

Amelia sighed, realizing that she would have to take another tactic.

"Very well, then," she murmured, closing her eyes and lifting her hands.

She focused all of her attention on the painting in front of her, picturing it in her mind, feeling the brush in her hand, the woman sitting in front of her as though she were behind the easel.

"Tell me your secrets," she said, trying to see within each stroke of the brush, and for a moment, she was there, in the painter's seat, watching the paint adhere to the canvas as though she was applying it.

She had been right. With her eyes closed, she could sense someone behind the painter's right shoulder, love emanating from him, although there was also hopelessness there, so intense that it threatened to rip her apart completely.

What had caused it? She turned, trying to get a sense of the identity of the man who had requested Isolde's painting, watching the brush strokes as though he wished he was caressing his fingertips over her skin instead, but she couldn't seem to turn completely around to see him.

*No*, she heard in her mind, but the more resistance she encountered, the more determined she became to see who was hiding from her.

"That's it," she murmured as she turned the other way, finding more flexibility there. She took a deep breath, turned, and then encountered what felt like a fist knocking against her head.

She gasped as her hands flew up to cover her temples, her eyes squeezing closed, her breaths short and fast as she fought the pain of what seemed like a strike.

Amelia backed up, trying to put as much space as possible between her and the painting – until she hit a solid wall behind her.

A wall who reached out and wrapped his arms around her, holding her steady.

"Careful, now," came the low-timbred voice, one that most certainly belonged to her physical world. "I've got you."

She whirled around to find the earl standing behind her, unease etched on his face as he looked her up and down.

She appreciated the concern, for she found that the world around her was growing dizzy from the magical knock to the head she had taken.

"What happened?" he asked grimly, and she wasn't sure how much she should admit. She stole a glance at him.

"I was trying to learn more about the painting, and I seem to have... hit a wall."

It was the truth, even if it wasn't complete.

"You appear to be in pain."

She rubbed at her temples.

"Somewhat. I was concentrating too hard, I suppose."

His gaze flickered from her to the painting behind her, and for a very brief moment, she saw lurking in his eyes, the very last thing she expected from him – fear.

"What can you tell me about this painting?" she asked.

"I've told you about it already," he said, his gaze hardening as he stepped back from her. "It is Isolde."

"Was she an ancestor of yours?"

He shook his head.

"No. My grandfather was in love with her, but of course, his father never approved of the match."

"Because she was a commoner?"

"That was part of it. She was a villager, well known for her many talents, including healing."

"She was a medicine woman."

"Most called her a witch, but yes. My great-grandfather was of the impression that she had cast a love spell upon my grandfather and was using him for his title."

"What happened to her?"

"Why do you think something happened to her?"

"There is true melancholy within this painting emanating from both Isolde and whoever commissioned it. If you would like me to do a proper job of this, I need to know all you can tell me about it and those involved with it."

"Very well," he said, looking back at the painting and then to her. "Come with me."

He picked up her tray, which was very un-earl-like of him, and led her out the door and into the adjoining drawing room.

"You do not want her to know that we are speaking about her?"

He didn't respond as he picked a bit of beef off her tray and ate it absentmindedly.

"My grandfather was convinced that their love was real, that it was too true to fabricate. Of course, I have no way of knowing for certain, but from the stories I've heard, he would have done anything for her."

"Even leave everything behind?"

His gaze shot up toward her.

"How did you know that?"

"I could see the love through the painting."

"Well, yes, I believe so. He told his father that he didn't care what he nor the family thought of the match – that he would marry her anyway and run away with her, leaving behind his family, his inheritance, and his responsibilities."

"Did he not follow through?"

"His father sent him on an errand, away from the estate for a couple of days – long enough for him to put his plan into place. My great-grandfather concocted a story, telling Isolde that his son had no love for her and that he had asked him to deliver a message to her, which he gave her in the form of a letter. Distraught at the loss of her love, she weaved a spell against the family. She was powerful, but the spell was so strong that, legend says, it took all the life out of her and she died right there on the steps leading into this house."

Amelia wished his story had come as a surprise, but she had already felt it, deep in her bones.

"Your grandfather must have been destroyed."

"He was," the earl agreed. "My family was never the same after that."

"Why not?"

He studied her momentarily before responding, as though considering whether she was worthy to hear the rest.

"My grandfather remarried as was arranged by his family, for he no longer cared what happened to him. It was a loveless marriage and after his wife bore a son, he died."

"Of a broken heart?"

"So they say."

"And Isolde remains."

The earl scoffed. "Are you telling me that you believe in ghosts?"

"Call them what you will," she said, waving a hand through the air before her. She was used to skeptics, but one would think that a man who lived with a spirit as strong as the presence before her would know more. "I can sense her, however. She is still not happy."

"You can say that again," he murmured.

"Do you have any other family that might be coming to stay in the near future who might know more?" Amelia asked.

"No," he said curtly, nearly before she had even formed the words. "They're all dead."

Her mouth dropped open wide.

"All of them?"

"All of them."

"What about cousins?"

"I have some distant cousins, I suppose, although none with any actual connection to my family."

"Friends?"

He shrugged his shoulders. "None worth noting. I try not to allow anyone too close to me. If I do… well, let us say that my family has not had a great deal of luck."

"Since Isolde laid the curse."

"I never said that it was a curse."

"You didn't have to," Amelia said with the smallest of smiles. "I already knew."

## CHAPTER 5

Max went to sleep that night more than slightly disconcerted.

When he had hired Amelia Lennox, he'd had an inkling that she had connected with the painting.

He hadn't expected her to read into it like she had.

Most of her suppositions could have been a guess, but she seemed to have an innate knowledge about his ancestors of which no one else was aware.

Max reached out to extinguish his candle, but before he could even pick up the tamper, the flame disappeared on its own. He shrugged, welcoming the assistance.

Like most nights, he lay back upon the bed, nearly too big for one man, an arm splayed out above his head. An arm that he knew was far too muscular for an earl, but his lifestyle as of late had been much more that of a laborer, for Max found that if he kept his body busy, his mind usually would be too.

He closed his eyes, blocking out the slight sliver of moonlight that shone in through the curtains, which he kept pulled back, for he preferred to wake with whatever sun chose to shine in the morning.

He had nearly succeeded in willing himself to sleep when a scream rent through the air, and he sat bolt upright in bed, throwing back the covers and then racing into the corridor, unconcerned with the fact that he wore only an old pair of very loosely tied breeches.

Max looked up and down the corridor before running to the balcony, peering over the railing and trying not to think of what had happened to one of his previous ancestors in this very hallway.

*In her bedroom.*

Without stopping to will the voice away – or to thank it – he continued down the hall until he reached Amelia's bedroom door, knowing which room the housekeeper had placed her in.

He knocked once, but when no answer responded, he pushed open the door and flew through it, likely looking the madman he was, standing in the doorway completely askew.

"Miss Lennox?" he called out, panting, seeing only a tangle of sheets upon the bed in the same moonlight that had encompassed his bedroom. "Are you well?"

The sheets flew upward as she sat up, a hand coming to her forehead. Her hair was unbound, long and dark around her shoulders, her dressing gown white and sheer, covering most of her body to where it tangled around her legs.

"My lord?" she said in a shaky voice, finally pushing back her curtain of hair to gaze up at him, her eyes wide and uncertain.

"What happened? Why did you cry out?" he demanded, and she squeezed her eyes tightly closed, confirming his suspicion it had been her.

"So much pain," she whispered. "She loved him so much and when she thought that he had abandoned her, she went wild in her grief. It ate her apart from the inside. She never thought he would leave her and when his father told her that

THE CURSED PORTRAIT

he had denounced her, she didn't believe it at first. But then she read a letter written in his own hand and found out that he had gone to court the woman he would eventually marry. It was too much for her to bear."

He didn't know what to say as he listened to the story, wondering if Miss Lennox was telling the truth or if she had become creative with the story he had shared with her earlier.

"Why did you scream?" he asked again, and she turned her eyes on him, finally focusing.

"That was the pain she felt when she learned of his betrayal. It was the pain that she put into the curse. And the curse... My lord, it is in the painting, and until it is broken, it will haunt your family forever."

Her lips were parted, her green eyes wide, and Max had to tamp down an unwelcome surge of lust that took him unaware. The woman was in a bed in his house, yes, but she was not for him. Far from it – for so many different reasons.

If that wasn't enough, he was a boor for thinking such a thing when the woman was clearly distressed.

Carefully, he stepped his way toward the bed, taking a seat on the edge, far enough away that he wouldn't accidentally touch her – to protect both her and himself, considering what had happened the last time their skin had brushed against each other's.

"Do you often, ah... see these types of things?"

Her eyes flew up to meet his, a touch of fear within them.

"It could have been a dream," she said, not answering his question. "After all that I learned today, all of the time I spent staring at that painting, the story must have been on my mind."

*She knows. She sees.*

He leaned in closer. "That's all you believe it is? Nothing more?"

"It is hard to say," she said, her expression shuttered, hiding away from him. "I should hopefully know more tomorrow after spending more time with the painting. Perhaps Isolde will see fit to share with me."

Knowing when he was being dismissed, he nodded, although he didn't seem to be able to take his leave just yet.

"Will you start working on the painting?" he asked.

"I won't actually touch the painting yet," she said. "I'll mix some colors, perhaps, and itemize all that I will need to complete it."

"I see," he said, peering closer at her, surprised to find a flush hiding on her cheeks, peeking through from behind her hair. "Are you sure you are well? Is there anything I can do to make you more comfortable?"

"No, but thank you, my lord," she said in a low voice. "Thank you for looking out for me."

"Of course," he said, forcing himself to stand. "I shall see you in the morning, then."

"See you in the morning."

He backed out of the room like a fool, but he wanted to drink in his fill of her. He might never touch her, but he would watch her for as long as he could.

When he fell into his bed just a few minutes later, for the first time in a long time, he fell quickly into a solid sleep, visions of a dark-haired beauty filling his head.

\* \* \*

THE NEXT MORNING, Amelia didn't even stop to break her fast before marching down the stairs and into the music room.

She needed to have a word with Isolde.

She crossed her arms as she stared at the painting.

"You can just tell me what happened!" she exclaimed. "No

THE CURSED PORTRAIT

need to send me into a panic in the middle of the night, causing the earl to come running into my room."

A very attractive, ruggedly handsome earl, she should add. One with muscles in places she didn't even know were possible to build them, who appeared so strong that she was sure he could pick her up and toss her over his shoulder with ease.

When he had burst into her room, shirtless, all she had been able to look at was that trail of hair that began at his chest and ran deliciously over his abdomen before stopping and finishing beneath his unfastened breeches below.

Just one small step and they could have come crashing down...

Amelia could sense Isolde's admonishment, and she shook her head at her.

"Just because you had a bad experience with a Blackwood man doesn't mean that I can't look," she hissed at her, glancing toward the doorway to ensure no one overheard her. "Besides, it is not as though I will act upon such lustful thoughts! The man is an earl. I know better – not that I am judging. I promise."

Did Isolde just tilt her head in understanding?

Amelia peered closer, deciding that it was time to take this a step further.

She had been pleased to discover that all of the supplies she had requested in her letter of response to the earl had been purchased and set out for her – including the easel. She sat down before it, stretching the canvas over top and setting out her paints in front of her.

She wasn't going to touch them to the Isolde's portrait.

She had something of her own to paint first.

Amelia closed her eyes, returning to the scene she had envisioned the night before.

It hadn't been a dream as she had told the earl.

She was certain that Isolde had been sharing a vision with her.

Her brushes swept over the canvas in front of her even as her eyes remained closed, the colors before her swirling of their own will before returning. They were mixed whirls of dark navy and purple and the black evil that Isolde saw in the man who had sealed her fate.

The truth of that night began to surface as Amelia learned the intentions and emotions of all who had been there.

She opened her eyes, returning to the present as the scene played out, coming alive off her painting, the figures taking shape before her and acting out the past in the music room around her. Isolde was in the middle of it all, her flaming hair spread out around her as though wind was sweeping through the room. The earl of that time was standing before her, an evil smile on his face as all that he had planned was coming to fruition.

And there, appearing at the door, was Isolde's lover.

He was trying to tell her the truth of it all, but she was so overcome in her pain that she refused to listen to any word that emerged from his mouth, and soon his pain became wrapped up in hers.

Amelia watched with wide eyes as Isolde chanted a curse, one that swept up all of the emotion and energy in the room, channeling it into the painting of her that was sitting near the side.

A painting that Amelia sensed from Isolde's lover was one gift he had planned to bestow upon her when he asked for her hand.

*"By the tears of a love unjustly torn,*
*And the blood of an artist's heart forlorn,*
*I invoke the powers of darkness and light,*
*To avenge this cruel and wrongful plight.*
*Upon the House of Blackwood, I cast this spell,*

*Until my story all do tell,*
*Misfortune and sorrow shall be your plight,*
*Endless as the darkest night.*
*The portrait of me, with pain imbued,*
*Shall hold the curse in colors true.*
*Each stroke of brush, each line and hue,*
*Bears the weight of love we knew.*
*Until the truth is brought to light,*
*And justice served to end this blight,*
*The heirs of Blackwood shall suffer the same,*
*In endless cycles of grief and shame.*
*Only when love and truth combine,*
*And past misdeeds are left behind,*
*Shall this curse be lifted, and peace restored,*
*To the House of Blackwood, forevermore."*

A spark flashed before her as suddenly the scene went black, the only remaining image was that of Isolde's lifeless body falling to the floor.

Amelia began to shiver as it all fled along with her own power, and Isolde's form slowly faded. Amelia had to step backward until the backs of her knees hit the chair behind her, and she fell into it with a thump.

It was only then that she realized she wasn't alone.

"My lord," she greeted the towering presence in the doorway, "How long have you been here?"

# CHAPTER 6

Max's breath had caught in his throat when he had first drawn closer to the music room.

It had nothing to do with Isolde or the painting. Instead, he had been intent upon the beautiful woman standing before the portrait, arms crossed, as though she was having a conversation.

Which she likely was.

Then she had started to paint, and Max couldn't look away, mesmerized by the intensity in her face and the way she seemed to be able to move her brush without thought, but only emotion.

And then she had stood, and it had all come to life before them.

He truly thought the madness had finally overcome him until he looked closer at Amelia's face and realized she was seeing the same.

In fact, she wasn't just seeing it.

She was creating it.

He had been so shocked that he hadn't said a word until

the apparitions all fell away and Amelia finally noticed him standing in the doorway.

"What in the hell was that?" he demanded, answering her question as to how long he had been there. Long enough.

"So, you have been here for a time then?" she winced.

"I most certainly have," he said, gesturing wildly in front of him. "Was this all some elaborate illusion?"

"Ah... *illusion* isn't the word I would use," she said carefully. "Perhaps you best take a seat."

He ignored her.

"Was that... was that the curse?"

"It appears so," she said, much calmer than his current state. "If only Isolde had listened to her lover."

"Edward," he said. "His name was Edward."

"Edward, then," she said. "She was just too overcome."

"How did you do that?" He set the curse aside for a moment. He had to know just who he had invited into his house.

"I suppose you could call it a skill of mine," she said cautiously. "A skill that is in the same vein of Isolde's curse."

"You are saying that you are magic?"

She stared at him, her green eyes wide, knowing, testing him.

"What if I was?"

"That can be a dangerous description for a woman."

"It *was*," she said flippantly. "Not so much anymore, although I prefer not to share the fact widely."

"Are you asking if I would keep such a secret to myself?" he said, sensing where her concern lay. "I can assure you that with the state of my family and the secrets we have kept for years, there is no cause for concern there."

She nodded slowly, although he didn't particularly like the way she was assessing him in turn.

He couldn't help but remember what had happened when

they had touched – had that been *her* magic causing such a collision?

"My lord?" she said slowly, yet with confidence as she did not break his gaze. "What is *your* power?"

His face turned into hardened stone as he stared down at her, immediately wishing that he could take back all that they had just shared, that he had just seen. He decided to answer in the most truthful way he could.

"I am an earl. I am more powerful than most Englishmen."

"Do not play stupid. That is not the kind of power to which I am referring."

"I cannot imagine any other that you could mean," he said, as foolish as he began to feel.

"This house – your family – there is magic here," she insisted. "Magic that combined with mine and knocked me over. You cannot tell me that you, the sole surviving Blackwood, do not possess any power whatsoever."

"Not a bit," he said.

It wasn't a lie.

He had no magic. He heard voices. That was it. He was a madman.

*You are not lying to her. You are lying to yourself.*

He never should have entered the music room. The voices were stronger here, to say nothing of Isolde herself.

"I need some air," he muttered slowly backing out of the room, a strange whooshing sound along with a breeze blowing by him as he did.

Goodness, what was going on here?

He strode through the drawing room until he reached the library, yet another room in this vast manor that had been woefully ignored over the past number of years. Max didn't stop to acknowledge Miss Lennox, who was matching him stride for stride as she followed him through the terrace doors and out onto the balcony beyond.

He started down the steps to the garden, where the vines had overrun most other vegetation. He swatted away an offending branch as he stomped over the ground so hard that it seemed to be responding to his anger.

"My lord?" Miss Lennox called out, even as he tried to ignore her. "My lord!"

"When I said I needed air, I meant alone!" he exclaimed as he whirled around, and a light wind began to swirl around him.

"The ground is shaking," she said, ignoring his ire as she pointed beyond him. "Look – it's from your steps."

"I hardly think I am strong enough to shake the ground."

"No," she said slowly. "But I think you can control it."

\* \* \*

HE STARED at her with such disbelief that Amelia knew he had no inkling of it himself.

"You must be joking," he bit out.

"The wind and the earth seem to respond to your words and emotions," she said. "I am not certain about anything else, and I could be wrong, but—"

"You most certainly are wrong," he said, walking toward her, even as the wind she spoke of whipped by his face, taunting him. "You are here, Miss Lennox, to do a job for me. Not to tell me that I am some magical being or that I must have supernatural powers. I told you – my power is from my station in life. That is all. When it comes to the painting, your job is to restore it so that it returns to a quality that will allow me to sell it. If you cannot do that, I will hire someone else."

Her head and shoulders dropped in defeat that she felt down to her very bones.

"Very well," she said. "Only, I don't think she will let you do that."

"Who?"

"Isolde. The curse is powerful and while its source is the painting, it extends over the entire house – the entire family. Selling the painting won't solve your problem."

"If the curse is within the portrait, and the portrait is no longer here, how could it continue?"

"You can try to remove the portrait, but it will find a way to return. The scene that we just witnessed included Isolde's curse," she said, her spark of interest returning. "She told us how to break it."

The earl strode over to her, lifting a finger and placing it against her lips, a slight spark filling the air between them, causing her to jump while, even still, he chose to ignore it instead.

"Shhh," he said. "Do not talk of breaking the curse."

"Whyever not?"

"Anyone who has attempted to do so before has met with an untimely end," he said. "Isolde does not want us to break it."

"But her words," Amelia insisted. "When she set the curse, at the end she said, *Until the truth is brought to light, And justice served to end this blight, The heirs of Blackwood shall suffer the same, In endless cycles of grief and shame. Only when love and truth combine, And past misdeeds are left behind, Shall this curse be lifted, and peace restored, To the House of Blackwood, forevermore.*"

"What does that even mean?" The earl said. "Truth brought to light. Love and truth combine. Past misdeeds left behind – it's all been done, and yet here we are, still caught up in the same curse. We know the past. We know that my great-grandfather was in the wrong, that Isolde and my grandfather misunderstood one another."

"Maybe it's the love part you're missing," Amelia said, walking gingerly around him and sitting on the stone bench beside him. "Have you ever opened yourself up to it?"

"No," he snorted. "What's the point? Everyone I love ends up dead."

"I am so sorry," she said softly, reaching up and cupping his face, tingles running from her fingers over his skin. She was beginning to realize where all of this animosity, especially toward magic and the curse, came from.

What would it be like to have all of one's family members and those most beloved taken from one due to a curse that was not of his own making?

"What about a woman who might love you?" she asked softly, but he was already shaking his head.

"I became close with a woman before, but nothing ever works out for me," he said bitterly. "I will spare you the details, but on the one occasion when I considered marriage, she soon found another much more suited to her. That is my life. At this point, there is nothing left worth saving any of this for."

"That's not true," she insisted, fighting the defeat in his eyes. "There is your own life. Your happiness is worth something."

"Is it, though?" he snorted. "What does it truly matter?"

"That's a very sad outlook," she said. "Everyone's happiness matters."

"Not mine. I—"

Before he could say another word, however, the slightly shaking ground that Amelia had noticed when she had first followed the earl outside was no longer just vibrating. It was beginning to quiver and tremble, like a giant beast awakening from slumber, its mighty roar deafening and its movements relentless.

Amelia met the earl's stormy grey eyes, knowing immediately that he wasn't the one causing this.

"Oh no," she whispered. "You were right."

He nodded slowly. "Isolde doesn't like talk of breaking the curse."

He grabbed her hand, pulling her toward the house, likely to seek safety, but Amelia shook her head, stopping and tugging on his hand to halt his steps.

He turned, disbelief in his eyes as he faced her.

"You can't keep running," she shouted over the noise of the earth moving beneath them. "You have to fight it."

"How could I possibly fight it?" he shouted as she gripped his forearms, holding him facing her.

"You can move the earth, I promise you can," she insisted. "Close your eyes and concentrate. Still the earth beneath your feet!"

He opened his mouth, about to argue, but then seemed to think better of it. Hope rose in Amelia's chest as he took a visible breath, squeezed his eyes shut, and did as she said.

Amelia gripped his arms, feeling the magnetic energy flowing out of her and into him, even through the linen of his shirt and the fabric of his jacket.

"Still it," she insisted. "Still it!"

For a moment, her heart beat fast in her chest as she waited for the earth to open up and swallow them both whole. Was this going to be her end? Was it due to a curse upon a family that wasn't her own?

She couldn't think like that. She needed to believe in the earl, for he didn't seem inclined to believe in himself.

She infused him with all of her strength and certainty, willing him to do what she thought he could.

And then, suddenly, all went still.

# CHAPTER 7

"You did it!"

Max came back to the present at Amelia's jubilant cry.

"I knew you could do it!"

He shook his head slowly as he looked around them, where the land had all returned to its former state as though nothing had happened, no threat had ever emerged.

It was as though he had lost consciousness for a moment, even though he was still upright on both feet, Amelia's grip holding him up.

"It's not possible," he murmured. "How could it be?"

"You have the power to speak to the earth," she said, squeezing his arms, much more thrilled about this revelation than he was. "Likely all of the elements, if I had to guess. Have you never felt it within you before – if you think beyond what you were trying to deny to yourself?"

He rubbed his brow. Sure, there had been the odd time when it seemed that his wishes or his whims came true when there was no reason for it, but it was never as though he felt any actual power over anything.

"I still doubt that I have control," he voiced aloud. "I—"

She shook her head, interrupting him. "I don't think you have control. I believe you can speak with them, urge them to do your will."

"That makes no sense."

"Not everything makes sense," she said with a laugh. "If it did, would we be here, fighting the spells from a curse?"

"No," he murmured. "I don't suppose we would be."

They stopped, staring at one another for a moment, her hands still on his arms.

"Is this what you truly want?" she finally said, tilting her face to look at him. A light dusting of freckles covered the bridge of her pointed nose, her eyes such a brilliant green that they nearly took his breath away.

He was about to answer that *yes*, he suddenly wanted her with a desperation that seemed to come from outside of himself, when he realized that was not at all to what she was referring.

"What... what do you mean?"

"Restoring this painting," she explained. "Isolde's portrait. Are you certain you want me to continue?"

He paused, considering her question before he nodded.

"Yes," he said. "If nothing else, *helping* her isn't likely to cause any issues, now is it?"

"That is true," she murmured. "Who knows? She might appreciate it. Very well. I will start without trying to see anything more about it. Although if Isolde wanted the truth known, you would think she would be happy that I showed the events of that night."

"Maybe she can no longer see the truth," he reflected. "Perhaps she has been so wrapped up in this curse that she cannot see anything beyond it."

"There is probably a lot of truth to that," she said. "Pain

has a way of overwhelming all of our other senses and masking most rational thought."

"I suppose it does," he said, dropping his arms abruptly. He did not want her to see that her words were just as true in his own experience as in Isolde's. "I must be going. I have tasks I must complete."

He tried to ignore the disappointment on her face at his words, but she simply nodded in return.

"I suppose now is as good a time as any to start working on the painting."

He turned toward the house but stopped when a thought struck him.

"Will you be safe working on the painting alone? Do you think Isolde might do you any harm?"

"Why, my lord, could you possibly be worried about me?" she teased, and he found himself both charmed and irritated at the same time.

"If you have any troubles, do not try to solve them alone. Come find me," he instructed.

The glint in her eye told him she didn't like being told what to do, but she nodded. He supposed that, as her employer, he had some say.

With a burst of energy, she charged past him, up the terrace steps and through the library doors.

"I'm sure Isolde and I will be just fine on our own, won't we Isolde?" she called out in a loud voice, leaving Max to sigh and roll his eyes. She needed to take this curse a lot more seriously, or they would all be in much greater trouble than she realized.

As he walked through the house and up to his bedroom, he could have sworn he heard laughter again.

Or maybe he truly was going mad.

\* \* \*

AMELIA SPENT the rest of the afternoon mixing the various powders and dyes with linseed oil, trying to determine how best to match the vivid colors of the painting.

She could feel Isolde watching her, and she chatted away as she worked, hoping to earn the woman's benevolence without raising her ire.

"Oh blast, there won't be enough for red," she murmured as she sifted through the powders before her. "I think the artist who painted you originally used carmine, but it fades too soon for my liking. Your hair, Isolde, needs vermillion. I shall muddle through with the first bit, as the carmine should work for the curtains."

Amelia reached for a quill pen and a sheet of parchment and began writing out her requirements before capping the pen and standing.

The ache in her muscles told her that she had been sitting for far longer than she had thought, and she stretched, reaching up to the sky before leaving the music room to find the earl and describe what she needed to complete the job. Although, she hoped he wouldn't ask her to explain why she needed additional canvas for her own works.

She started her search in his study, but when that came up empty, she continued on to the drawing room and then the library. When she still found him missing, she asked one of the maids to see if the butler was free, and Whitaker appeared momentarily.

"Whitaker! I was wondering if you might know where I could find the earl?"

"He is working outside, miss."

"In the gardens?"

"I would venture beyond the gardens. Last I heard, he was fixing a fence."

"I see," she said, even though she was slightly confused. Since when did an earl fix his own fence? Perhaps she did not know the actions of the nobility as well as she thought she did.

"He will return by dinner if you would prefer to speak to him then," Whitaker said, and Amelia nodded her thanks, but she rather liked the idea of taking a walk outside. It was not a particularly sunny day, but the overcast sky would be pleasant, and she could use the exercise after sitting for most of the day – after their brief dance with an earthquake, of course.

She decided to take the same path they had walked earlier, and this time, without the distraction of the shaking earth, she appreciated the charm that could be found even in the overgrowth. It might not be perfectly trimmed and cultivated, but she could see the beauty in the foliage of each leaf, each plant, even each acorn scattered across the ground.

As she walked away from the manor, she wished she had the foresight to have asked Whitaker in which direction this errant fence could be found, but she figured she would walk until she reached a fence and then follow it along until she found the earl. How large could the property be?

Soon enough, the overgrown hedgerow widened until the greenery became less of a garden and more of a woodland. She closed her eyes, allowing her senses to guide her as the chirping birds and the rush of the breeze around her soothed her spirit. As she tuned into her soul instead of her mind, she fixed her focus on finding the earl, and her feet began to lead her west, away from her current path.

Unafraid of becoming lost, she allowed her intuition to guide her, and soon enough, she broke clear of the forest and found herself in a meadow slightly inclined upward. As soon as she crested the small rise in the land, there, in front of her, was exactly who she had been looking for—the earl, doing as Whitaker had said, fixing the fence.

Only, she was about to be blessed with more than she had ever planned for.

There was the earl, yes. Fixing the fence by himself.

She was also, however, receiving a full view of him shirtless, uncovered except for the pair of breeches he wore, as he had been the night he had burst into her room after her dream. Only this time, he was swinging a hammer over and over again. With each swing, the generous muscles of his chest, shoulders, and biceps tightened and swelled, leaving nothing to her imagination.

His face was etched in concentration, sweat running in droplets from his temples.

Never had a man appeared more alluring.

Amelia's mouth turned dry as she watched, and she began to feel that she was intruding on a moment she should have no part in.

She took a step backward, about to retrace her steps, when the earl looked up, apparently sensing her movement.

"Are you going to stand there watching all day, or are you going to come help?"

"Help?" she repeated as she began to take slow, disjointed steps down the hill toward him.

"Help, yes," he said with what could be described as the hint of a smile gracing his lips. "Or did you have another reason for seeking me out? Did you need some entertainment?"

Suddenly, her requirement for more paint seemed like a trivial excuse for having come to find him all the way out here in the middle of the day. Surely, she could have waited for dinner, as Whitaker had suggested.

"I was out for a walk," she lied, and he lifted a brow as though he could see right through the excuse, although he blessedly didn't comment upon it.

"I see," he said, grunting as he swung the hammer again.

"Hold this," he said, setting a fence post upright. She took it between both hands, trusting that he wouldn't miss his target when he swung again.

She held on tight, her body jolting with the force of his pounding, but she was proud that she was able to hold the post steady.

"I must ask, why are you doing this?" she said. "It does not seem like a typical task for a man of your station."

He stopped, lifting a piece of linen from the ground below him and wiping his brow before returning his attention to her.

"It is not," he said, "But I suppose I am not a typical earl."

When he didn't continue, she pushed on.

"So you like this type of activity?"

"You could say that," he said, before swinging again. "I like to do physical labor, because—" swing "—then my mind doesn't get away from me."

Well, that was intriguing.

"Tell me more."

"You are aware that I am the one paying you, are you not?"

"I am aware, yes. I would still like to know if you would agree to tell me."

"Fine," he said, apparently giving up on his job and dropping his hammer, leaning against a fence post he had already successfully slotted into the ground. "If you must know, here it is. When I work with my body, I can ignore what is happening in my mind."

"Which is?"

He swiped at his brow. "I never thought I would share this as I didn't want anyone to think me mad, but something tells me we are already far past that point."

She couldn't help but chuckle. "I have heard more in my time than you would believe, my lord."

"Such as?"

She paused, wondering how much she should share. She wasn't about to tell him the secrets of anyone within her society or put their meetings in danger, but she also realized that she might need to share a secret with him to earn his trust.

"What if I told you that I know a fair number of people with magical abilities, each unique? They come about differently in different people, but many of us have found each other so that we do not feel quite so alone. It is not like the days of the lone persecuted witch any longer. And, I should add, I know just as many men with abilities as women."

He studied her for a moment, as though wondering whether or not to believe her, but she could tell when he decided to trust her by the look of resignation on his face.

"I hear voices in my mind, all right? They are stronger when I am at the house – either of my houses for that matter. When I get away and do something physical, they are silenced. They drive me mad."

Amelia inhaled at that, further intrigued when he would no longer meet her eyes.

"How interesting," she said, leaning in closer, becoming more in tune with the masculine scent emanating from him. Another's such scent would likely disgust her, while his caused desire to unfurl within her belly.

It was a wanting that she had never felt before.

"Interesting?" he repeated. "It's madness."

"*Who* is speaking to you?" she asked, ignoring him.

"Who? I don't know. A voice. Conjured from my own head."

"I doubt it," she said, tapping her finger against her lips and shaking her head from side to side. "Have you tried asking?"

"Talking to the voice?" he said in disbelief. "No. I far prefer to ignore it."

"Well, next time," she said, tilting her head to the side with a smile, "try asking the voice what it wants. That should help."

He shook his head at her. "I never should have told you."

She began to back up the hill, feeling that if she stayed, she might be more tempted by him than she should be. He was an earl, her employer, and now she was finding too many reasons to want him more than she should.

"You probably shouldn't have," she agreed, lifting her voice so he could hear her as she stepped farther away.

"Why not?"

"Because you know that I will not leave you be about this now," she said, laughing. "I cannot wait to hear more, my lord!"

And with that, she turned around and scampered up the hill, leaving the earl and all of his sweaty, tantalizing masculinity behind her.

## CHAPTER 8

Max sat at the dining room table, lost in thought, his fingers tracing the intricate carvings on the old oak surface. The flickering candlelight cast dancing shadows across the room, adding an ethereal quality to the atmosphere. He couldn't shake the feeling of vulnerability that had opened within him after he had revealed his secret to Amelia. Now he wondered what consequences might arise.

*You did the right thing. Finally.*

What if she could read his mind? That was a frightening thought.

When he finally opened his eyes, sitting across from him was Miss Lennox, having snuck into the dining room as silently as a spirit herself. Her green gaze, soft and understanding, met his.

As much as he knew he should likely be asking her to leave his manor so that he could hire someone far more suitable who would simply do as he or she was told without causing mayhem, Max couldn't help but be drawn to her.

At the moment, he was distracted by the way her long

dark hair framed her face like a halo in the dim light, not pinned up around her head like the style of the day.

Despite the unease swirling within him, she had a comforting presence that soothed his restless soul.

In that fleeting moment, Max felt a sense of connection that transcended words.

It was as if they were two halves of a whole, bound by fate and entwined in a spell woven by unseen forces.

The very last thing a man like him, who preferred to remain unencumbered and alone, desired.

The timeworn walls of the manor seemed to hold their breath as they waited for one of them to speak. Amelia's eyes mirrored the flickering candle flames that danced with a life of their own.

Max's eyes were drawn to the delicate curve of her lips, slightly parted as if on the brink of revealing a secret. His hand moved involuntarily across the table, reaching toward hers as the air around them crackled with an unspoken tension.

Just as their fingertips tentatively touched, a sudden chill swept through the room, extinguishing the candle flames in a swift gust of wind. Shadows lengthened and twisted, contorting into eerie shapes that seemed to whisper forgotten secrets. Max's hand gripped Amelia's as the temperature dropped drastically, casting a frosty veil over what had promised to be a comfortable dinner just seconds earlier.

Amelia's gaze darted around the room, her eyes curious and concerned. Max steeled himself, ready to provide her with all the protection he was able to conjure.

As the candle flames flickered back to life with an otherworldly blueish glow, a low murmur filled the air. It was a haunting melody, ancient and sorrowful, resonating with a power that defied logic as shadows swirled around them like wraiths, sending a chill up Max's spine.

"Has it ever been like this before?" Amelia whispered, reminding him that they had not spoken since she had appeared at dinner, even though it seemed their emotions were intricately intertwined.

"Yes," he muttered. "The night before my mother died."

\* \* \*

Amelia took a breath, her gaze flickering around the room.

They couldn't let something like *that* happen again; that was for certain.

She had many questions, but they would have to wait.

While she could admit that she had become rather invested in the Earl of Blackmore and this curse that had been laid upon his family, she wasn't about to lose her life over it.

Fortunately, she had a few weapons of her own.

She stood so quickly that her chair tumbled backward.

"Stay here," she said before running out of the room as quickly as she could, sensing the earl's questioning gaze upon her.

But all he had to do was keep himself safe long enough that she could do what she needed. She thanked the stars above that she had mixed paints earlier that day while simultaneously bemoaning that she would have to redo it all to match the colors exactly.

But no matter.

She held her skirt out in front of her to fill it with a paintbrush and jars of paint before she ripped a sheet of canvas off the easel and ran back into the dining room, where she threw it all upon the table, which was still empty aside from their wine glasses.

THE CURSED PORTRAIT

It seemed that angry spirits prevented servants from carrying out their duties.

"What are you doing?" the earl called out as objects began to fly about the room. He ducked to prevent his own spoon from whacking him across the head.

"Just wait," she said, lifting a finger. Realizing that the canvas would fly around the room if she used any inanimate objects, she lifted it and placed the corners in his hands. "Hold this," she instructed.

He fixed her with a look of disbelief although he did as he was told while she dipped her brush into one of the pots before stroking it across the page.

She worked quickly, effortlessly, closing her eyes and allowing her hand to fly as she painted with her soul. It would not appear to be anything particularly worthwhile, but that was not the point of this – the point was to calm the spirits that surrounded them, namely that of Isolde.

She stepped back, placed the brush down, and with a whispered incantation, she lifted her palms and sent all of her intentions into the painting before stepping back, allowing it to come to life.

The earl dropped the canvas entirely when the lovers, wrapped in an embrace, began to float off the canvas and hover in the air between them, but it didn't matter. Her work and its purpose was complete. In the middle of the dining room, the beautifully landscaped garden that Amelia had painted, complete with its vibrant flowers and lush greenery, sprang to life.

Amelia had been inspired by the meadow near where the earl had been working earlier today, and she could only hope that it was such a place Isolde might have remembered, especially in a time when it had been kept up to the standard it deserved. At the center stood the lovers, one as dark and as handsome as the current earl himself, the other with flaming red hair, albeit in carmine instead of vermillion, their love for one another evident in their gentle smiles and the tender way they held one another. Their figures were blurred, giving them an ethereal, almost ghostly quality, symbolizing their love that transcended time.

The wind that had battered the dining room began to subdue as the entire room became bathed in a soft, golden light, adding a warm, nostalgic glow to the scene that Amelia hoped was something akin to a memory.

She was so focused on the tableau coming to life before her, wondering if it had been enough, that she didn't realize the earl had circled behind her until his hand touched her shoulder.

"You did it," he whispered in awe. "You've calmed her."

She blinked and looked around the room. The candles were lit, but not with the harsh flame of before. Instead, they had returned to their gentle orange glow, while all of the objects that had flown around the room were returned to their places as if nothing had ever happened. Amelia still sensed Isolde's presence, but it was softer now, subdued.

"Thank goodness," she whispered.

"I don't know how you did it, but somehow you understood her pain and transformed it," he said, his eyes still on her creation, apparently mesmerized.

"I was trying to remind her of the happy times she experienced with your grandfather before the betrayal," she whispered, not wanting Isolde to hear and feel she had been manipulated. "I wanted to remind her of the love that had once filled her. It was what she said could be the key."

"You were right," he said, his hand still warm on her shoulder, his fingers inching closer to the bare skin of her neck.

"My lord?"

"Yes?" he said.

"I think I'm going to need more paint."

* * *

Hours later, when their dinner was finally finished, Max found he couldn't move from his place at the table. He could have spent all night sitting and watching Miss Lennox.

She was awe-inspiring.

He had doubted her abilities, as well as what she thought he was capable of wielding.

But her powers were breathtaking.

Her powers and her own understanding of how to use them. He wondered what else she could do but was honestly too afraid to ask.

"You're scared of me now," she ascertained, breaking the silence as she ran her fingers over her wine goblet, and he wished she was stroking his skin instead.

"I'm not scared of you," he insisted but then paused. "I'm slightly scared of what you can do."

She laughed softly. "I do not use my abilities for harm. Well… not too much harm."

He eyed her. "What's that supposed to mean?"

"I have done things I am not proud of to survive."

"Such as?"

"You will think less of me, my lord."

"Just call me Max."

"Max?"

"I think we have been through enough together to become familiar. I fear we will not have time for you to call out 'my lord!' during Isolde's next attack."

She chuckled.

"Very well. And my friends call me Amelia."

"Amelia." He liked the way her name rolled off his tongue.

"I promise not to think less of you, no matter what you tell me. *Friend*."

She scrutinized him before rendering him trustworthy enough to continue. "There have been times when I have used my powers to afford my rent."

"How did you do so?"

"By painting things that convinced people to pay me money for them."

"I would pay you a fortune for what you just did!" He paused. "If I still had a fortune."

She smiled. "That is kind of you. But that is not entirely what I mean. I do not show most people my powers like I just did. I can also simply paint a picture and infuse it with emotion that passes to whoever is viewing it, causing them to part with money simply because they have suddenly discovered they want to."

"Interesting."

"I'm not proud of it."

"We all do what we have to do sometimes."

She tilted her head as she eyed him across the table, while some of the closeness that had been present before Isolde's attack came creeping back between them.

"Do you say that from experience?"

He passed a hand over his face, trying to determine just how much to share with her.

In the end, he decided all of it. Why not, at this point?

"After my birth, which was apparently the one miraculous moment of my family's lives, my mother was unable to carry another child. Then my mother died."

"What happened?" Amelia asked quietly, sensing that he needed to speak of it; that, perhaps, he never had before.

"She fell from the balcony," he whispered, the pain flashing across his face.

"Oh, Max, I'm so sorry," she said, reaching out and taking his hand in hers.

He shook his head as though ridding himself of the emotion. "It was a long time ago. We don't know if she was pushed or if it was an accident or what exactly happened. Then my father died as well – from an accident that I barely survived myself."

"Is that how you got this?" she asked, tracing the scar that ran through his eyebrow.

"Yes," he said. "Who knows where the bit of luck came from that I was thrown far enough to escape the crush of the carriage that took my father. After that, I did what I had to in order to survive. There was no money left behind. Every bit of it my family ever touched might as well have been set on fire the way it disappeared. I've gotten by through selling various estates, items, and land. There is no use investing or trying to have a solid crop. It all comes to naught."

"There is nothing wrong with selling things that belong to you."

"My ancestors might think differently."

"Are you living for them or for you?"

He bowed his head, her question surprising him, for he had never thought of it quite like that before.

"Both, actually," he said quietly. "I think I feel as though I owe them something."

"Why? Because you are the only one still alive?"

He met her eyes. "Yes. That's basically the way of it."

"I see," she said, flattening her palms upon the table as she stood, surprising him. "I have a suggestion, then."

He nodded, desperate for any counsel – especially from her.

"Do *that*, then."

"Do what?"

"*Live.*"

# CHAPTER 9

Amelia knew that her declaration had shocked Max, but perhaps that was what he needed—someone to knock him out of the rut he had fallen into of always waiting for the worst to happen.

She did sympathize with him. His life was worth more than a curse that had not even been his fault.

But it was up to him to break it and find a way to make atonement for his family's sins.

For, as he said, there was no one else left to do it.

Amelia would do what she could to understand Isolde and her curse, but she knew she couldn't do it alone. They needed help.

Help she sensed Max could acquire if he would give in to the powers that were begging to be released, but he was still far too stubborn.

In time.

In the meantime, over the next few days she mixed the remainder of her paints as she awaited new arrivals.

This time, her list had included plenty of extra so that she would be in no danger of running out were she to need them to go on the offensive again.

She rather hoped that Isolde would cooperate.

Amelia did, however, have another painting she needed to work on before setting to work with Isolde.

Max was clearly hurting.

He needed his spirits cheered – and she knew just how to do it.

Closing her eyes and casting her mind over the acres of land and what she knew of the grounds, Amelia tried to decide where he would find the most joy.

Perhaps it was outside because of his choice of manual work, but where?

Finally, it came to her, and she closed her eyes and began to paint.

A few hours later, she had just set down her paintbrush when Max's broad shoulders filled the doorway of the music room. He pretended that his visits were conducted out of interest in her work, but Amelia was well aware that he was checking on her – and perhaps on Isolde.

Instead of being annoyed, however, it was actually rather comforting to have his visit to anticipate.

"How is progress today?" he asked in clipped tones, and she smiled to ease his discomfort from opening himself up with such vulnerability the previous evening.

"Slow, but we are getting somewhere," she said. "The colors are nearly perfect. I do wish I knew a little more about Isolde herself, but I do not think that I am going to solve that problem today."

"No, I gather not, although I feel as though we probably know too much already," he said, leaning against the door frame, watching her. "Were you painting yourself?"

"I was," she said, suddenly concerned about what he

might think of her artwork. She stood up, stepped back, and waved a hand toward the canvas.

"For you," she said.

"What is for me?"

"This painting."

"Is this part of a nefarious plan to convince me to give you all of my riches? Because I can assure you there are nearly none left."

"No," she laughed at his look of trepidation. "This painting isn't for anything. It is just for you to enjoy. If I had wanted to steal from you, I would have done so already."

"How reassuring," he said dryly, coming to stand beside her, likely so that he could better examine the painting.

"What do you think?" she asked, putting slight pressure on the small of his back and urging him forward.

"I think..." he began before stopping and pausing for a moment, truly taking in what was in front of him. Eventually he turned to her, his eyes wide. "I think that it is beautiful."

"Truly?" she said, her heart beating faster.

"Truly," he agreed, stepping forward and stopping right in front of it now. His breath caught slightly. "It feels...." His voice lowered to a whisper. "Joyful. How I remember my childhood, from before I lost my parents."

She could have sworn he was choking back tears, not that he would ever actually allow them to fall.

"It's my family," he finished with a sense of completeness.

She nodded. "I hoped the likeness would be close enough. It's the three of you, sitting on a blanket in the grass. Of course, I do not know what your parents looked like, so I decided I would use silhouettes instead."

"How did you know which backdrop to include?"

"It's part of the landscape beyond what I would assume to be your bedroom window. It looks over the grounds, which presumably were well maintained at the time, a place where a mother would endeavor to take her child."

She could see the joy flowing out of him, both practically and spiritually. It was exactly what she had wanted – to add a touch of happiness to what had become a rather depressing life.

"Take it," she said softly, sensing that he didn't want to be vulnerable with her once more and open himself up to his emotions. She leaned forward, waving her hand in front of it, using her powers to dry the paint to the canvas, before she unfastened the clippings, and passed him the unfurled canvas. "Do with it what you will. It's a gift."

"You are the one with the gift."

She ran her hand along his face, surprised at how comfortable it felt to do so.

"Thank you," she said. "You have one too. Don't be afraid to use it."

And with that, she released him and he slowly backed out of the room, canvas in his hands.

\* \* \*

MAX PACED BACK and forth down the drawing room floor, wondering if he was wearing holes into it.

He couldn't stop looking at the painting Amelia had created for him. Why had she done it?

He was mustering up the courage to ask her when a yell sounded in the direction of the library, and he took off as quickly as he could to find the source.

He was unsurprised to find Amelia standing before the door of the music room. It was the wall of fire that took him off guard.

Instead of a doorway between Amelia and the music room, flames licked the wall. While they didn't seem to be burning any material, heat emanated from them, and he had to stifle the urge to reach out and grab Amelia to pull her back to safety.

"Isolde," she said calmly, hands held up in front of her. "I am only trying to enter for my paints. That is all."

"Amelia, back away from that thing!" he shouted, and she looked back in surprise.

"It is only Isolde," she said with a sigh and a roll of her eyes as she placed her hands on her hips as though she was chastising a child. "She is trying to prevent me from entering."

"Why?" he asked, wondering why he was even entertaining this mad conversation between Isolde and Amelia, but knowing he had no choice now.

"She thinks I am a danger to her portrait. I promise you, Isolde, I am not."

*You want my secrets and my curse.*

"I do not. I want to help you."

Max blinked. He had heard Isolde many times before, but he never realized that Amelia could actually talk to her as well.

Odd.

"Amelia. Back. Away," he said through clenched teeth. "I will find servants and we will—"

"You will do nothing," she said firmly. "That will only scare her."

"I am not going to stand here and watch a wall of flame attack you."

"She won't attack me."

A lick of fire burst out and shot right by Amelia.

"She's just trying to scare me," Amelia reasoned, and Max sighed. If Amelia wasn't going to see reason, then he would have to show it to her.

"Amelia—"

Before he could make it all the way to her, however, Isolde began casting even more fiery bursts Amelia's way. They both dove to the floor to escape them, Max throwing his body over Amelia's.

As her soft body huddled beneath him, a strange sensation of coolness poured over him, beginning from his back and growing out from around him. When he finally risked a look above him, he was shocked by what he saw.

He and Amelia seemed to be hiding within a watery bubble, one that he hoped wouldn't pop until this fire was finished, for it seemed to be rejecting Isolde's flames.

"What did you do?" he called out to Amelia, but she wrinkled her nose from her position beneath him.

"*I* didn't do anything," she said. "*You* did!"

"This looks like it is protecting us."

"That's because it is." Her green eyes shone toward him, giving him far more credit than he deserved. "You created a protection spell. A ward – using the elements. It seems that water will bend to your will as well."

"How?"

"When you threw yourself over me, you were thinking of protecting me. It must have triggered it," she said before her expression softened. "Thank you."

"Thank *me*, after everything you have done for me so far?"

"Woefully nothing as of yet, I'm afraid."

"As lovely as this is, do you suppose it is time we concern ourselves with this massive fireball in front of us?"

"Most likely," she said, her eyes calculating. "We have two options."

"I'm listening."

"First, we paint our way out of it – except that my paints are beyond the fire, which I'm sure Isolde well knows. Or… you battle it."

"Alone?"

"I'm here," she said. "I'll help you as I did before and infuse you with as much of my power as I possibly can. That worked before."

Determined, Max nodded, the weight of the responsibility to, most importantly, see Amelia through this safely, resting on his shoulders.

He wasn't sure he believed that he had the power to take on an angry spirit, but Amelia's belief would have to be enough to buoy him forward.

She fit her much smaller hand into his larger one, squeezing it to urge him on. Using his other hand to lift her up with him, they rose within their protective bubble, Max with newfound resolve.

*She's right. You can do this if you actually believe in yourself, although that would be a first.*

Max was about to tell the voice where it could shove itself but, remembering Amelia's words, took a breath and decided that perhaps he just might ask it a question instead.

*What am I supposed to do?*

*Solve the problem. Connect with the fire. Use your power to speak to it, not to control it.*

Max nodded and steeled himself in front of the wall of flame as energy coursed through him, emanating from their joined hands. From Amelia.

Drawing strength from her magical abilities, power surged within him, and Max stood undaunted as he faced the crackling flames roaring higher than any fire he had ever seen.

Closing his eyes, he reached deep within himself, searching for any hidden reservoir of strength.

With a steady hand and a focused mind, Max used that same mental pathway he spoke to the voices in his head with and began to search for the fire, as ridiculous at that felt.

Wisps of magic danced around his fingertips as he crafted a counterbalance to Isolde's fiery onslaught.

*Embers*, he thought, picturing the fire fading to nothing, and when he opened his eyes he was shocked to find that while the fire had not yet retreated, a swirling vortex of water and light was beginning to form in front of him.

"The fire is Isolde's," Amelia's voice called out. "You cannot affect it – unless it is through your own elements. You are on the right path."

He nodded, reaching out and using a hand to move the vortex closer to the fiery wall until it was right before it.

The fire seemed to hesitate, as though it was unsure of what to expect – and then Max sent the water crashing through it.

His heart stopped for a moment as he waited to see the result of his actions. The water clashed against the flames, creating a steamy barrier that hissed and crackled with energy. Max held his breath, fearing that he had only further angered Isolde.

But to his surprise, the wall of fire began to sizzle and shrink back, as if recoiling from the onslaught of water. The room filled with a hissing sound, and slowly but surely, the flames diminished until they were nothing but flickering embers on the floor – just as he had pictured.

Max watched in awe as the last remnants of fire faded away, leaving behind only a faint wisp of smoke in the air. He turned to look at Amelia, who was gazing at him with a mixture of relief and admiration in her eyes.

"You did it," she whispered, her voice tinged with awe.

Triumph and relief washed over Max in equal measures. He had never felt such a rush of power before and knowing that he had protected Amelia filled him with a sense of accomplishment unlike anything he had experienced.

They had been connected from the very beginning, yes,

but their joined effort to overcome Isolde strengthened their bond to one that he couldn't quite put into words.

As they stood amidst the dissipating mist of the extinguished flames, Max couldn't help but feel a newfound respect for Amelia's abilities—and a fair bit of jealousy at her belief in herself and what she could accomplish.

Amelia stepped closer to him, her hand still clasped in his, a smile playing on her lips. "I knew you had it in you, Max," she said softly, her eyes searching his. "I think you are more powerful than you even realize."

Max was at a loss for words, his mind racing with the events that had just unfolded. He could harness his own elemental power to protect other people? Unbelievable.

Until tonight, he would have said it was impossible.

"We make quite the team, don't we?" Amelia said softly, her gaze meeting his with a warmth that sent a shiver down his spine.

"We do," Max replied, only right now he didn't care about spells or curses or even the fact that Isolde's portrait was sitting there on the other side of what had been, moments ago, a wall of fire.

He didn't care that he was an earl on the brink of ruin due to a curse that was entirely based on a love affair between two people from very different stations.

All he cared about were Amelia's very plump, very pink lips.

Lips that were currently caught between her teeth, setting his every nerve on edge.

*Kiss her.*

He wanted to tell the voice to shut up.

But for once, it had a very good idea.

## CHAPTER 10

Max towered above her, the strong lines of his face illuminated in the soft flicker of candlelight. The hush of the room was filled only with the echo of their breathing and the crackle of dying embers.

His gaze was fixed on her lips, and she wanted very much for him to lean in all the way and meet their mouths together.

Amelia's heart raced as Max's warm breath brushed against her skin, his hand gently cupping her cheek. Anticipation, hesitation, and longing all seemed to merge together into a single moment of suspended time.

And then, as if drawn by an invisible force, they each crossed the distance halfway and their lips finally met.

It was a gentle touch at first, tentative and uncertain, an exploration of the desire that had been simmering between them ever since they met. But as their kiss deepened, a surge of that undeniable passion ignited between them, binding them in a dance of raw emotion and unspoken truths.

Amelia melted into the embrace, losing herself in the intoxicating sensation of Max's lips moving tenderly yet urgently against hers. The world around them faded away, leaving only their synchronized heartbeats and warmth that enveloped them together.

Each brush of his lips against hers sent sparks through her veins, as heady and powerful as any spell.

Amelia could taste the lingering sweetness of magic on his lips, feel the gentle pressure of his hand against her cheek, and hear the soft cadence of his breath mingling with hers.

As they broke free from the kiss, their eyes locked in a silent exchange that spoke volumes beyond words. Max's gaze held a mixture of reverence and adoration, as if he had discovered a hidden treasure in the depths of her soul. Amelia, however, felt that *she* was the fortunate one, for Max's kiss had opened a hidden chamber within her, where emotions long kept at bay now surged as hot and fiery as Isolde's spell had been.

The echoes of their kiss reverberated through Amelia like a long-forgotten melody. With trembling fingers, she reached up to caress his cheek, feeling the stubble beneath her touch, grounding her in the reality of the moment.

Max's eyes bore into hers, a silent question hanging between them, pleading for permission and understanding. In that shared gaze, Amelia saw reflections of her own longing.

She nodded slowly in answer to his question.

Yes, she wanted this. Wanted him. As much as he was willing to give her and for as long as he would keep himself open to her.

"Max," she breathed, "should we—"

"We... should say goodnight," he said, his face suddenly shuttering as he stepped backward as though he was closing a door between them. Amelia's heart fell, even though she knew that his dismissal had nothing to do with her — it was due to all the reasons he told himself that he couldn't be happy or find any joy.

"Very well," she said, forcing a smile she didn't feel onto her face. The swirling passion deep in her stomach was telling her to fight for this night with him. But the truth was, he was probably right. He was her employer, and she was supposed to be spending months here. How would she do so if they became intimate and he pushed her away *after* that? "Goodnight, Max."

She walked away regretfully, feeling his gaze on her back as she went.

* * *

MAX WAS PROUD OF HIMSELF.

He had shown great restraint, stopping himself before he and Amelia had taken any rash actions that might have been brought about by the rush of excitement after quelling the dark forces.

So why did it feel like he had made the worst decision of his life?

He tossed and turned all night. Every time he closed his eyes, all he could see was Amelia's face, backlit by a wall of fire. Then, a deluge of water seemed to douse him. When he woke, his entire body was wet, and it appeared that his dreams had come to life.

Perhaps he never should have given in to these powers that had been tugging at him for years now.

They had saved Amelia, yes, but now he had no idea how to live with them.

He needed help.

He hated that he had to ask, but after he had continued on his fence work that morning, he sought Amelia out in the music room, where today, she was actually sitting in front of Isolde's painting, her brush touching the canvas.

"Here for your daily check on me?" she asked without turning around, and he watched her side profile, loving the way that her tongue peeked out of her mouth, touching the corner of her lips in concentration.

"I don't check in," he argued, and she peeked over her shoulder toward him.

"You do. But it's fine. I actually look forward to seeing you."

He grunted awkwardly, unsure of how to respond. She was so much more forward than most women of his acquaintance that he often wasn't entirely sure how to speak with her.

"I need your help," he blurted, unsure how else to ask.

"Isolde seems to be behaving herself today," she said. "But what can I do to aid you?"

"It has to do with these… powers that I seem to have."

"That you do have," she corrected. "Not that you seem to have."

"Very well, that I have," he corrected, stopping himself from rolling his eyes. "I don't know what I'm supposed to do with them."

"*Do* with them?" she repeated, continuing to paint. Only he wondered how she was making any progress, for every time she brought her brush to the canvas, it was only to make the smallest dots or strokes that he couldn't even see. "You use them."

"Well, that's the thing. I don't know how to use them. They present themselves at inopportune times. I need to control them."

"That's your problem right there," she said. "You cannot control them. You have to learn how to live in harmony with them."

"Will you help me?"

"How would you like me to help you?"

"To... practice, I suppose." He ran his hand through his hair, and she must have sensed his frustration for she finally turned around and studied him more closely.

"I would be happy to help you with whatever you need," she said. "We can practice."

"Tonight?" he asked, pushing away from the doorway, sensing that she was focused and didn't want to be disturbed at the moment.

"Tonight. After dinner," she agreed.

He was sure this was going to make for a night to remember.

He just wasn't sure what type of memory it was going to be.

* * *

AMELIA'S entire body was cracking with anticipation over the rest of the day.

She could hardly believe that Max was embracing his powers. He had not only used them but had wanted to learn how to work with them.

Quite different from the man she had first met, who had refused to believe in magic altogether. She supposed living with a spirit who had cursed your family would be one way to convince a person.

They didn't speak of it during dinner, instead discussing her work on the painting and his on the fence.

When they stood afterward, his face was drawn, likely hiding any nervousness he was feeling.

"Let's go to the terrace," he said. "There is nothing important out there that I might destroy."

"If you believe you are going to destroy something, then

you will," she said. "That's the first lesson. You have to believe in yourself and your abilities. If you don't, no one else will."

"Except you."

"Except me." She smiled as he held his elbow out to her. She took his arm, reminiscent of that first night they met, as he led her through the library doors and then outside, where the night air greeted them, cool and crisp.

The moon hung low in the sky, casting a silver glow over the cobblestone path that wound through the estate's unmanicured gardens. As they walked in silence, the only sound was the soft rustle of leaves in the breeze and the distant hoot of an owl.

She stole glances at him from the corner of her eyes, his profile sharp and defined in the moonlight. There was mystery to him, depth that she couldn't quite grasp, a piece that he was still holding back from her.

They reached a secluded garden bench, the sides of it adorned with climbing roses that had been allowed to grow of their own will, their sweet scent mingling with the earthy aroma of damp grass.

Max tugged her hands down to sit on the bench and then turned to face her, his eyes searching hers with an intensity that made her breath catch in her throat. "There is something I must tell you," he said, his voice low and serious, causing her heart to race.

She lifted a brow and waited for him to continue.

"I'm nervous," he admitted.

She released her own uneasy laughter that his revelation was not particularly disturbing.

"That's understandable."

"Do you think you could tell me how you first discovered your powers?"

"Of course," she said, happy to do so if it would help him

feel more comfortable, sinking closer into him, her thigh pressing against his.

"I was still fairly young—only ten years old. We lived in London, not well off but with enough to get by and be happy."

"That sounds like a nice upbringing."

"It was." She smiled as she reminisced. "My mother was a painter, and I painted with her for as long as I can remember. One night, I was in the middle of painting, and you can imagine my shock when the dog I had painted came to life and started running around the room barking at me."

"You are not serious."

"I am. I was both thrilled and terrified. I had always wanted a dog of my own but not exactly in that way. Fortunately, my mother had always been a medicine woman herself, and she was no stranger to what she called witchcraft. It was in her family, and she had been watching to see if it was something that I might inherit."

"So, she knew how to help you."

"She did. There are even societies in London where people with abilities gather and help one another. She introduced me to one of them who has been of great help to me."

"How fortunate I am to have you, then," he said dryly, but she answered him as though he was being serious, patting his leg.

"You are, actually."

"What do we do first?"

"The first thing you have to do is to talk to this voice of yours in your head," she said, causing him to rub the bridge of his nose.

"I'd rather not. He's annoying."

"Maybe he thinks the same of you."

Max laughed at that.

"Very well. Here we go."

# CHAPTER 11

Max closed his eyes, exhaling slowly.

"What do I even say?" he asked Amelia.

"Say you're sorry for being rude in the past and then ask him who he is and what he wants you to do."

Max bristled, his eyes popping open. His life had not prepared him to spend much time apologizing or explaining himself. "Do I have to?"

"You don't have to do anything, but you asked for my advice."

She had him there.

"Very well."

He closed his eyes again and focused, picturing the voice in his mind.

*Looking for me?*

*Yes.*

*Something you'd like to say?*

*Damn it.*

*I am wondering who you are.*

*Anything else you are supposed to say first?*

*Fine. I...apologize for ignoring you in the past.*

*Ignoring? Or rudely telling me to leave you alone?*
*Perhaps a bit of both.*
*Very well. I will accept your reluctant apology.*

"What did he say?" Amelia whispered.

"That he accepts my humble apology," he said, while the voice in his head snorted.

"If you have done your apology, you can ask who he is now," she whispered, as though that would prevent this voice from hearing them.

*Care to share your identity with me?*
*Do you care to know?*
*I asked, didn't I?*
*Very well. Shall we make a guessing game of it?*
*I'd rather not.*
*You're no fun. Very well. I am your grandfather.*

Max's eyes shot open. He supposed he should have realized it, but he had been alone for so long, his life void of any other family members, that he never guessed that one would still be around… in one form or another.

*Surprised you, did I?*
*You could say that.*
*Why wouldn't you have told me?*

He opened his eyes to meet Amelia's gaze, so intently green in the moonlight as she waited patiently for him to return to her.

"It's my grandfather," he said.

Amelia's eyes widened, but that wasn't what shocked him. It was the glass shattering in the house beyond.

*That's why.*

"Isolde." Amelia's eyes met Max's as her mouth rounded into an O. "This is not good," she said before lowering her voice. "Ask him how he feels about her."

"No!"

"Just ask. Maybe he can help."

"Very well," he grumbled.

*Are you and Isolde still... friendly?*

*You can tell that beautiful devil—*

"No," he said, cutting off his grandfather. "No, they are not. I'd call it... a love-hate type of thing. He isn't happy about the curse."

Amelia stood, pulling Max to his feet.

"I think we're going to have another lesson pretty soon," she said, looking around them, wary for danger. "Now that you have allowed your grandfather to truly communicate with you, the rest should come easier. We know you can speak with the ground, air, water, and fire. We learned last night that you do not just move elements, but you can conjure them as well. With any magic, your mind is the most powerful part of it. You need to believe and command with confidence. Do you see that rock over there?"

She pointed at a rock about the size of a hand across the path, and Max nodded. "I do."

"Move it."

"Where?"

"Anywhere. Just move it. Focus on it and where you want it to go."

He nodded and stared at the rock, focusing all of his attention on it. He thought about lifting it, and, ever so slowly, it began to shake until it was moving across the path to the other side where he had wanted it.

"That's good, "she said. "Now, see if you can send a trickle of water over it."

"Water from where?"

"That is up to you."

This one was harder. If he could focus on an object or something already existing, it was easier. Any other time, he had actually created something from nothing; it hadn't been on purpose but more either in a moment of panic and desperation or in response to something else.

He stared at the rock, picturing it wet and glistening.

Then, shockingly, a small shining fountain appeared from nowhere and water began trickling down overtop of it.

"Very good," Amelia murmured, reaching over and squeezing his leg. It made him want to continue to please her so that, hopefully, her hand would continue to inch up higher.

A sudden gust of wind whooshed between them, and Amelia looked at him immediately.

"Is that from you?"

"No," he shook his head. "It must be Isolde."

*That would be her.*

*How long is she going to continue these attacks?*

*As long as there is a curse.*

*Should we actually consider breaking it?*

*It will take a great deal from both you and your woman. Sacrifice and vulnerability.*

*But is it possible?*

*It is.*

He had been so focused on the conversation with his grandfather that he hadn't noticed what Amelia had been doing. She had worn a bag around her shoulder, and she pulled it out now, arming herself with paintbrushes and a small piece of canvas.

"What are you doing?"

"I'm preparing," she said, and as she did, the trees around them began twisting, changing from harmless, beautiful greenery to something far more sinister, the branches becoming looming arms stretching toward them, the gnarled trunks their bodies, notches in the tree becoming sinister faces.

"How do we combat this?" Max said, staring at them,

trying not to turn and run away. He had lived at Blackwood Manor for years but had never seen anything quite like this before. How much damage could a tree do?

One of them lumbered forward, its roots ripping out of the ground and stomping slowly along the path like a stiff upright octopus. As it began its slow, menacing stride toward them, one of its branches reached out. Max ducked, and it hit the bench where they had been sitting moments before, sending it flying onto its side.

Quite a bit of damage, apparently.

He turned, ready to shield Amelia, but she was crouched on the opposite side of the path, furiously painting.

He stood over her, ready to battle for her, although how, he wasn't entirely sure. Then she lifted her canvas to the sky and showed a silent, starlit night with a circle of calm, inanimate trees surrounding it. She closed her eyes and then whisked it off the page and into the air. The colors from the painting blended and swirled in the air as they began to wind their way around the trees, stilling each of them as they wrapped around them.

Finally, all of the monstrous trees stopped their lumbering and Max breathed in a sigh of relief as he watched Amelia, who was now tucking away her paints as though nothing had happened.

"Is this a regular occurrence for you?" he asked, and she laughed.

"Not entirely. But sometimes our group is called on to provide assistance when a spirit such as Isolde has taken over a property, and we do what we can to help."

"So, you *have* done this before."

"Yes. But not alone."

"You're not alone," he said, taking a step toward her and lifting his hand to her cheek. "You have me."

\*  \*  \*

Amelia's heart started pounding at his touch, her skin tingling where his hand cupped her.

"I actually believe we might have a chance at breaking this... you know," he said.

"You can have a future," she said, spreading her fingers over his chest. "You are worth having a future."

"For right now," he said, his index fingers trailing a line over the bones above her eyes, "why do we not just focus on tonight? On the time we have together?"

"That is just fine with me," she said, biting her lip as she took his hands and interlaced their fingers together. "Shall we go inside?"

"Did I practice my magic enough?" he asked, arching a brow, and she had to bite the inside of her cheek to keep her full smile from blooming.

"I can think of other ways to practice," she said suggestively, and he chuckled as he followed in behind her.

They kept their hands intertwined as they walked up the wide staircase until they reached the corridor above. When they began to walk toward Amelia's room, Max tugged on her hand.

"My room is much bigger," he said as he led her down the hall and then pushed open the large oak doors.

Amelia's breath caught when she walked through. While it was obvious that very little in the room had been replaced in years, it must have been absolutely majestic at one point.

Everything was black with gold trim. The bed canopy and covering appeared to be shiny black silk, while all of the paintings and furniture were trimmed in gold, even if some of it was beginning to fleck off.

"Your great-grandfather styled this room, didn't he?" she said, and Max turned to her in surprise.

"How did you know?"

"I'm not sure." She shrugged. "Just a feeling. And it seems like it would suit such a man."

"I've never felt particularly comfortable here, but I also haven't had any resources to change anything," he said, looking around him, unaffected.

"Maybe it would be a good idea to try," she said. "I doubt Isolde has any wish to have reminders of your great-grandfather in the house, and if you are not particularly fond of the décor, then why not change some of it with furnishings from elsewhere?"

"I could try that."

"I could paint something on the walls for you if you'd like," she said. "I promise that you would have the best sleeps."

"I can think of another way to help my sleeping," he said, reaching out and drawing her close. Amelia's breath caught as she nearly trembled before him at all of the promises that the throatiness of his voice held within.

"That helps you fall asleep?" She tilted her head to the side as she studied him. "It usually only wakes me up for the night."

"Usually?" His eyebrows rose, and Amelia, who hardly ever felt any shame, felt warmth rushing up her cheeks. He must have sensed it, for he shook his head and leaned in, placing a kiss on her forehead. "Nothing to be ashamed about."

"It was only a handful of times," she said. "One of the men from our committee. I—"

"No need to explain," he said, shaking his head. "It is not as though I am telling you my entire history, am I?"

"You are not."

"See? It doesn't matter. All that matters is you and me. Tonight. Together."

"Well, look at you, my lord. It seems that you are a romantic."

"No one has ever accused me of that before."

So often throughout her life, Amelia had to hide a part of herself – her artistic side or her magical side – but with Max, she felt as though she could truly be herself, allowing him to see all of who she was and what she was capable of.

His gaze was intense, his eyes burning with a passion that set Amelia's heart racing. He took a step closer, reducing the distance between them in one swift motion. Amelia's breath hitched as his hands fitted around her waist, pulling her closer still. His skin was heated, the pounding of his heart matching her own.

Slowly, deliberately, Max leaned in, his lips meeting hers in a kiss that was at once tender and fierce. Amelia responded in kind, her hands reaching up to tangle in his hair.

She knew at that moment that she would remember tonight for the rest of her life.

## CHAPTER 12

The air between Max and Amelia was charged with anticipation. Every detail of the room faded into the background as his focus centered solely on the woman in front of him.

Her presence was a force to be reckoned with, and he found himself utterly captivated by the way her eyes sparkled with their hidden depths of passion and intelligence. The delicate curve of her neck, the soft rise and fall of her chest with each breath – all of it seemed to call out to him in a way that was impossible to resist.

He had tried to deny her and their chemistry, but after how they had opened up to one another tonight, he finally decided that he had no choice but to give in. It seemed that forces were going to pull them together one way or another, so they might as well enjoy it.

As he pulled her closer, a surge of desire unlike anything Max had ever known pulsed through his entire body. The weight of responsibility that usually burdened his shoulders fell away in that moment, replaced by an intense longing for something more primal, more real than anything he had thought was possible.

Their lips met in the age-old dance, each movement echoing the unspoken words that passed between them. Max savored the taste of her skin as his hands explored the curves of her body with reverence, silently promising her protection and desire with his every touch. The room seemed to shimmer with an otherworldly light, casting their entwined forms in a halo of shadows and whispered secrets.

Amelia's gasp melted into the kiss, her fingers clutching at his shirt as if grounding herself.

Max moved deliberately yet achingly gently, almost fearing she might disappear if he held her too tightly. His heart thundered in his chest as he deepened the kiss, pouring all his longing and need into it.

Her hands roamed over his broad shoulders, and he had never felt as strong as he did beneath her touch. She traced the lines of his back as if committing him to her very soul.

Max wove his fingers through her unbound hair, tugging gently to expose her neck to his kisses. His breath was ragged against her skin, and she arched into his touch with a soft whimper. He slowly unfastened each button on the back of her dress, somehow finding calm within his storm of emotion as he completed each one capably.

"Max," she murmured, and when he looked down at her body beneath his, he nearly choked. Her fingers were colored in what appeared to be paint, and as he watched, she almost glowed before the colors began to become unattached from her fingers, flowing off their tips like cascading colorful waterfalls.

"Amelia, you are... incandescent," he said with a swift intake of breath. Her eyes were closed, her head thrown back, and he wasn't even sure if she was aware of just what her body was doing.

Not that it mattered.

When he tried to remove her arms from her sleeves gently, she surprised him by shrugging out of the garment with grace, the rainbow trails of her fingers reaching out and wrapping him in their warmth before practically plucking his own jacket off of his body.

Even the way she undressed him was an art form. As soon as all of his garments were on the floor at their feet, her dress, stays, and chemise followed suit.

Max had seen – and even owned – many works of art in his life, but he had never seen anything nearly as breathtaking as an undressed Amelia.

"Amelia, you are a masterpiece," he breathed, and she answered by running her arms down his chest until she wrapped them around his waist.

"I want to paint you," she said in response, her fingers trailing over the muscles of his chest. "Would you let me?"

"I have a few other things I need to do at this moment," he said in a low, throaty voice. "But I will give you anything you ask for."

She captured his lips again, her hands coming around his head to hold him close and steady as she kissed him with more passion than he was aware could be contained within a woman.

He could do nothing but return it in equal measure before he leaned down and placed his arm beneath her knees, lifting her and carrying her over to the bed without breaking their kiss.

He set her down on top of the blankets, but she was anything but demure.

Instead, she placed her hands on his chest and used her legs to flip them over so that she straddled him. She crawled up his body, running her fingers over every bit of him, leaving colorful streaks in her wake. Every time they touched, it was like a new miniature explosion, and he was fearful for a moment about what would happen when they actually came together.

But not fearful enough to stop.

She trailed her fingers down his chest, over his hips and thighs, and then when she leaned down and took him fully in her mouth, he nearly fell over the edge right there. He threw his head back as he opened himself up to her, ready to grant her anything she asked for.

"Amelia," he groaned. "You have to stop. We need—I need—I want you fully. Beneath me."

His need to claim her was stronger than any emotion he had felt before as he lifted her in his arms and laid her on the bed. Her eyes glazed over as he reached down, slipped a finger inside her to make sure she was ready for him, and then slid inside her, finding home.

After his initial thrust, he had to pause for a moment, for he was nearly overcome by the greatest sensation of righteousness he had ever felt.

She gripped him tightly, clutching him close to her, until he finally had the wherewithal to begin moving.

Every thrust was more exquisite than the last, their bodies intertwining in perfect harmony. They moved, in accord and perfectly in tune, the world falling away around them.

Gone was any thought of a curse, of the future, of the fact that they came from completely different worlds that could never become one.

Their bodies didn't care—nor did their souls, which had merged together until Max didn't know where he ended and Amelia began.

Their lips locked, passion-filled and desperate, the sounds of their moans mingling with the creaking of the bed beneath them.

Amelia's fingers dug into Max's back as their bodies moved together, each kiss and touch sparking new life into the flames of their desire. Her green eyes, now dark with passion, never left his face, and he was absolutely spellbound by her and the way they had come together. Max felt as if he were drifting, his senses heightened to the point of transcendence.

"Touch me, Max," she breathed, her voice husky with longing. "Show me what you can do."

Her words sent a shiver down Max's spine, and this was one challenge he most certainly would not back away from. He complied with her wish, gently cupping her, his thumbs brushing against delicate flesh while his fingers danced across her in a hypnotizing rhythm.

Amelia's breaths quickened, telling Max that his touch was eliciting the desired response. She arched her back, inviting him closer. Through their locked gaze, her eyes, wide and full of emotion, pleaded with him to take her further.

Max's eyes narrowed as he took in her request, his own desire beginning to peak. With a breathless growl, he increased his pace, his hips moving in a powerful, possessive rhythm. Her moans echoed through the room, mingling with the sound of their own panting and the creaking of the bed, as if they were the only two souls left in the world.

Amelia's fingers dug deeper into his back, urging him on, her voice strident with need and longing. "Harder, Max. More. Please."

Max, unrelenting, gave her what she wanted, his thrusts becoming more forceful and intense. The air was thick with the scent of their arousal, their bodies slick with sweat as they moved together. Amelia wrapped her legs around him, her toes curling with pleasure, her nails digging into his back as she cried out his name, her voice echoing through the room.

As they reached the crest of their desire, Max could feel the magic within him begin to surge, the energy of their connection becoming more profound with each passing moment. There was no control left as he let go of everything, giving it all to her. He knew there was danger in unleashing his power in such a vulnerable moment, but the desire to claim her completely was too strong to resist.

With a roar, Max released the magic within him, power coursing through his body and mingling with Amelia's. The room was filled with a brilliant light as their bodies intertwined, the energy between them creating untold power. For a moment, they were suspended in time, their souls connecting, transcending space and dimension.

As the energy dissipated, they lay there, panting and spent, their bodies still entwined. Amelia's emerald eyes met Max's gaze, and he saw the same hunger and passion he felt reflected back at him. There was no need for words, for they both knew that what had just happened was more than mere physical pleasure.

It was a bond, a connection that neither of them could have foreseen. One that Max didn't see any way of breaking out of. Nor did he want to.

Perhaps he had been right in trying to avoid this – for now that they had come together, there was certainly no going back.

Slowly, Max pulled away from Amelia, though his eyes never left hers.

"We should get some rest," he said softly as he tenderly cupped her face.

"We should," she agreed before a cheeky smile crossed her face. "We'll need our energy to do that again."

He groaned as he lay back and flung an arm over his face. "I can hardly wait, but I'm going to need some time."

When he set his arm back down, he blinked as he suddenly noticed his surroundings for the first time since they had come together.

Gone was the faded black and chipping gold that he so hated. In its place was a kaleidoscope of color, but, strangely enough, not the bright rainbow that had trailed from Amelia's fingers, but instead, strong, rich colors, those which would have suited his own palette. They were painted in a mural of color that he realized was the very grounds from beyond the manor, brought in to adorn the room.

"Amelia," he murmured. "Look around."

She lifted her head lazily, blinking when she saw what surrounded them.

"My goodness," she said with a swift inhale. "Where did this come from?"

"From you," he said in amazement, but she shook her head.

"Not from me alone," she said. "I have never done anything like this before. This comes from both of us together. A merging of our abilities. Don't you see? It is a painting, yes, but of all the elements that matter to you."

She lay back against him as they stared at the room around them, the air between them charged with a comfortable sense of magical calm.

"Max?"

"Yes?"

"Do you think that perhaps... *this* is what is needed to break the curse?" She flipped over and stared at him, her chin resting on her fists. "That it's not just one person's magical ability, but a coming together of two – of the two of *us*?"

Max had thought that he was supposed to spend the rest of his life alone. He had always known that the curse would end with him, but maybe... just maybe, it would end with him in a different way.

"It could be," he finally agreed. "But how?"

"That is what we have to discover," she said with a grin. "Why don't we start tomorrow?"

"Tomorrow?"

"Yes," she said confidently. "Because we have much more to do tonight."

## CHAPTER 13

Amelia had never felt so sated and yet also so certain that she was exactly where she was supposed to be, doing exactly what she was supposed to do.

She was meant to have come here, to Blackwood Manor, and to meet Max.

She was bound to him in a way that she couldn't explain. She just didn't know whether it was for now or forever.

But Amelia was not one to make plans for the future. She preferred to take things day by day, for she had discovered long ago that plans often never resulted in the way she envisioned them.

She had spent the entirety of the previous night in Max's bedroom, cocooned in a curtain of magical protection. When they had come together, so had all of their abilities, in a mixture of color, elemental magic, and a shield of protection that kept them safe from any curse or other threat.

But they could not stay hidden in a bedroom forever, as much as both of them would like to. And so, this morning she had risen with renewed purpose to determine just how they were supposed to find the answers to breaking this

THE CURSED PORTRAIT

curse and its hold on Max and his family – present and future.

"What do you think this is going to accomplish?" Max asked as they walked through the halls of the manor. Every time they passed a painting, Amelia paused, closed her eyes, and touched her fingers to the canvas, trying to read into it.

"I'm trying to see if any of the paintings might provide us a clue on how to break the curse," she said. "Perhaps while I am doing this, you could ask your grandfather."

"He won't speak of the curse," he said, shaking his head. "I can understand why."

"Ask again," she urged. "Just one more time."

He looked at her from the corner of his eyes before sighing and taking her hand. "Very well."

*Can you tell us more about how we break the curse?*

Amelia jumped at the voice in her head. She looked at Max and dropped his hand, the voice going silent. She took it once more and the voice resumed. Her breath caught. She could hear the voices through her physical connection with Max.

*You're on the right path. Find my portrait. The answers are there.*

*It would be a lot easier if you just tell me.*

*I cannot.*

*Why not?*

*It is part of the curse itself. But remember that such an act does not come without great sacrifice.*

"He said that we have to find his portrait."

"I know," Amelia whispered. "I could hear."

He seemed surprised but accepted the news. "Follow me."

He led them down the grand staircase, past the study and the library, until they emerged in what would have been a small ballroom at one point in time. Amelia paused, admiring the statues that stood sentry in the doorway.

"It's in here?"

"Yes. Once we stopped hosting balls, the family began to use this room as an art gallery. It's where many of the paintings are stored."

He led her into the room, a musty air surrounding them. Amelia wondered when anyone had last actually used it.

It was, however, the place where all the art that had been showcased in Hampstead Heath had been returned. She could see that those pieces were not as dusty as a few of the others.

Since none of those statues or paintings had called to her there, she ignored them as she followed Max to the portrait in question.

"This one," he said, pointing to a portrait near the back of the room. It featured a man who looked something like Max, although his hair had a curl to it, the hardness in his eyes catching Amelia off guard.

The portrait was set against a backdrop Amelia recognized as the drawing room of Blackwood Manor, which still held the same heavy crimson drapes and dark wood paneling. Painted around him were subtle signs of power and legacy, including the family's coat of arms and a grand fireplace that she was not certain was actually present in the room.

Max's grandfather stood regally before it all, his commanding presence exuding confidence. His face toward them was stern but fair.

She noted that he wore a family signet ring on his right hand, and a watch chain peeked out of his waistcoat pocket.

"This was a different painter than the one who painted Isolde," she murmured, sensing Max moving in closer to her side. "The lighting is warm and dramatic, and there is still a rich color palette, but more muted. The textures are meticulous, but much different than in Isolde's painting. This was painted to showcase his power, unlike Isolde's, which was painted to show the love that someone had for her."

"I am certain you are correct," Max said. "My grandfather's portrait would have been painted by the same artist who did all of the family's. I believe my grandfather privately commissioned Isolde's."

She stopped, sensing the charge emanating from the portrait before she even put her hands to it.

"He's a handsome man," she said with a look back at Max, whose lips began to turn upward until they descended into a frown. "He liked that, didn't he?" she laughed, sensing that his grandfather must have had something to say to Max about her comment.

"Not much he can do about it as I'm the one still alive," he snorted, and Amelia rolled her eyes before returning to the painting. "Well, Grandfather Edward," she said. "Let's see what you have to say for yourself."

A thought struck her as she considered how strong her abilities had become when combined with Max's, and she reached out and took one of his hands in hers before she placed her other one on the portrait.

"Here we go," she murmured as she closed her eyes and surrendered to the painting and whatever it had to show her.

Whenever Amelia saw into a painting, it was not a surprising thrust but rather a gentle welcome into the world beyond it. She sought out the story she was looking for, asking Max to help her by asking his grandfather to guide them. She sensed his reluctance, but they broke through, and soon enough, the man who had been standing motionless in the painting came to life, walking in front of them.

Amelia couldn't have said whether she was seeing him in her thoughts or whether he was truly walking the floors of Blackwood, but to her, he was as real as Max himself beside her.

"Welcome to Blackwood Manor," he said, his voice low and otherworldly. "You fit in well here, Miss Lennox."

"Thank you," she said simply, waiting for him to continue. She had always found that spirits liked to be given the time to speak, for it had been so long since they'd had an audience to do so.

"What answers do you seek?"

"The curse," she said, sensing a rumbling from beyond her even just upon saying the words. "We want to know how to break it."

The spirit nodded as he looked first to her and then to Max, who appeared to be standing right next to her.

"You know that is a dangerous ask."

"Do you know the answer?"

"I do," he said. "I was there when most of the curse was cast."

"We know," Amelia said. "We heard the curse being cast as well. What we don't know is how to break it. Isolde never said anything about how to do so."

"She said that love was required."

"We did hear that."

"I already told my grandson here that you must make great sacrifices if you want to do this."

"What does that even mean?" Max interjected. "I have nothing left to give."

"Do you not anymore?" his grandfather said, his eyebrows raised as he looked in Amelia's direction.

Amelia's heart began to beat faster. If his grandfather felt that they meant something to one another, could Max's feelings for her be as strong as hers for him?

"Very well," he continued. "If you need all of the steps on how to go about this, then here is what you must do. The first concerns the portrait itself. Miss Lennox should continue to restore it. Within the painting, you will find hidden symbols and incantations that are crucial for breaking the curse."

Amelia wished she was able to write all of this down, but she would just have to remember it.

"Then you will need Max himself and the abilities that he has finally recognized. If he channels fire, water, earth, and air, he can surround the portrait and the ritual site with a protective spell."

"Ritual site? Where is that?"

"Where it was cast, of course."

"The music room," Amelia breathed. "Of course that is where it would be."

Max's grandfather wasn't finished yet. "Maximillian, you have finally learned to embrace the voices inside your head. You have this young lady to thank. Do not shy away from that ability. You will need us now more than ever."

"To do what?" he asked.

"To help you. To talk to you. All you need to do is stop closing us out."

"Very well," Max grumbled.

"Finally, the curse will require sacrifice from you. Some of it is physical sacrifice. You must find something that was meaningful to Isolde, and you must also be willing to give away all of your powers as you bring the past to light and look forward to the present."

"Give away all of our powers?" Amelia asked, and Max's grandfather harrumphed.

"The curse will only mean something if you are willing to give every part of yourself – emotional, physical, spiritual."

Amelia's jaw went slack at the words, for she knew that a spirit was not going to lie – he was truthful about everything he said, meaning that the breaking of this curse could be more than she had ever bargained for.

"No," Max said, stepping forward powerfully, placing an

arm in front of Amelia in a gesture that was both incredibly annoying and yet also admirable as well. "I am willing to sacrifice parts of myself for this, but Amelia should not have to do so. She came here only to restore a painting, not to break a decades-old curse and lose something of hers in the process."

"Do you not think that is for me to decide?" Amelia asked drolly, lifting one of her brows.

"I do not want you to do it for me," he insisted, and Amelia felt a small piece of her heart die at that. For the more time she spent with him, the closer to him she was drawing. She would do this for him, yes, but because she saw a future together with him. She had no idea how long that future together would be, but she wanted to fight for him.

Perhaps that was the only option here. She would rather see him live a happy, curse-free life, even if it was without her in it.

She squeezed their hands where they were still interconnected.

"Let me give you this one last gift," she urged when she noted that his own face was shuttered.

"Even if it takes everything from you?" he said.

"I am sure there are ways around it," she said. "But I do not back away from a challenge, and I am willing to take on Isolde." She tugged on Max's hand and they stepped back, away from the painting. "It seems that we are on our own. Your grandfather spoke in circles. But there is one thing that I have taken away from that for certain."

"What's that?"

"I must work on Isolde's painting. And I must do it sooner rather than later."

"What am I to do in the meantime?" Max sounded helpless.

"You practice and you perfect your abilities. Speak with the elements. Weave protection spells. I know you can do it."

"And if I can't?"

"You *can*. I've seen you do it. Open yourself up and allow the magic to flow through."

"Very well," he sighed, stepping backward and looking around him as though he had forgotten where they were. His grandfather had returned to the painting, apparently having imparted all of his knowledge.

"Well," Amelia said, turning and beginning to walk away from him, hips swaying from one side to the other as she went, "I best begin my work on this painting. Wish me luck."

"You don't need luck," Max called out after her. "Not when you have everything else you'd ever need."

And, buoyed by his belief in her, Amelia squared her shoulders and went to find Isolde. She was going to break this curse. She just had to ask for a little bit of help first.

## CHAPTER 14

Max leaned against the doorway of the music room, watching Amelia work. She was mesmerized by the portrait in front of her, almost as though she was in a trance. Max guessed she basically was.

She had been determined to finish her work as quickly as she could in order to break this curse. Every morning, she broke her fast and then sat in front of Isolde's portrait, her brush on the canvas as she highlighted every detail of the backdrop, the pieces scattered over the table in the painting, and, of course, Isolde herself.

It had been days since they had used their powers to speak to his grandfather through his portrait.

She broke from her work late in the evening to eat dinner and they spent every night together in Max's bed. It was still more magical than it had ever been with another, but Max felt there was something missing between them since that first night — like she was not completely present with him in the moment but rather part of her was elsewhere.

He knew exactly where she was.

With the painting. With Isolde.

He appreciated Amelia's dedication, and yet, he would prefer to have all of her. It scared him to think of the sacrifice his grandfather had referred to. If this was what she was like working on the painting, what would happen if she had to sacrifice even more of herself?

"Amelia," he said softly now, hoping to give her a break for a time. When she didn't answer, he raised his voice slightly. "Amelia."

She started and looked around as though she didn't know where she was, before she blinked a few times, her eyes coming back into focus.

"Max," she said with a slow yet slightly absent smile. "I didn't see you there."

"I know," he said, walking into the room and leaning down to cup her cheek. No matter how many times they touched, it still shocked him that every time they did, tingles trickled over his skin. "You've been working hard. Do you want to take a break?"

She looked from him and back to the painting. "I should keep going."

"Amelia, I appreciate what you are doing, but you cannot allow this painting to take over you," he said as gently as he could. "If we don't break the curse, then we don't break it. It's not worth losing you to it."

He heard a rumble from the piano across the room that he knew was Isolde voicing her displeasure that he was offering an opinion. There hadn't been any more incidents since Amelia had started to pay such dedication to the painting. Apparently, it was keeping Isolde happy, but the spirit didn't seem pleased with Max's interference. She wanted Amelia all to herself.

"She wants me to finish the work," Amelia whispered, confirming his suspicions. "But…" She looked from one side to the other before standing and grabbing Max's hand, tugging him to stand with her. "Come with me."

She led him through the library and out the terrace doors, walking them so far from the house that he wondered if she was going to take him to a neighboring property.

Finally, she seemed happy with the distance and stopped.

"What is it?" he asked, unable to wait any longer to know what was so bothering her.

"It's Isolde," she said, her nose wrinkled in distress, her green eyes searched his imploringly, as though she could find all the answers to her concerns in his eyes. "I feel that the more I work on her painting, the more she is... I don't know... drawing me in. I have never felt this before. In the past, whenever I have worked on enchanted paintings, while they have told their stories, I have never encountered a curse that is so wrapped up in a person and a painting as this one."

"You should stop," Max said immediately, shaking his head. "This was my concern. I do not want anything to happen to you because of this job. I—"

She placed her hand on his chest, interrupting him. "Don't you understand that this is more than a job to me now? I need to do this. Not only do I not want to leave you with this curse alone, but I also feel that it would be too difficult for me to break away. There is only one way through and that is to finish this. But I need your help."

"Anything," he said, realizing that he truly meant it. He would do anything to keep her safe. He wished now that he had never drawn her into this. He had naively thought that this would be much easier — that he could restore the painting and be rid of it and the curse. But he would never have known the truth of what had truly happened if it wasn't for Amelia, nor would he know that the curse wouldn't leave him even if the portrait did.

Amelia seemed to think that this was how it should be,

but he couldn't believe that, if it meant any harm would come to her.

She looked at him imploringly, gripping his hands. "I need you to make sure that I don't lose myself. That I do not allow Isolde to take me over."

"Why do you think that would happen?" he asked urgently.

"I can feel her calling me, as though she wants something from me," she said, despair trickling from her voice.

Fear gripped Max's heart. For he could see it. It was what had been keeping Amelia from fully giving herself to him, and yet, until now, he had tried to deny it. It was why he had felt that it wasn't the same as it had been between them that first night.

"I don't know what she wants aside from her portrait being complete. I don't know if she knows that by doing this we are trying to break the curse. All I know is that she wants something, and I need you to keep her from taking me with her."

"Do you think that's it?" he asked. "Do you think she wants to use you somehow?"

"I don't know. She would have to be one of the strongest sorceresses I have ever known if she were to do so, but it is not outside the realm of possibility."

"Amelia, I don't like this," he said, shaking his head, clutching her arms, not realizing how tightly he was doing so until she winced slightly, and he loosened his hold. "There has to be another way."

"There isn't," she insisted. "Not that I can see. Will you help me?"

"Of course," he said. "That isn't a question. What do you need me to do?"

"Just be there with me. Do what you did today and check in on me. Don't let me become too caught up in the work."

"I can do that," he said resolutely. "Have you learned anything else?"

"I have seen more into the curse, into what she was feeling. Her pain has only increased over the years. The curse has grown her power, which has been fueled by the dark emotions she used to create it. The way through is to show her that love is possible, that there was love there for her from your grandfather. Somehow, we need to cut through that hurt."

"Do you have an idea how we can do that?"

"In addition to working on her portrait, I must work on my own painting. One that I will infuse with all of the emotion that I believe is needed to break it. Then we will use that along with all of the other elements possible and your own power to set up a ritual to break it."

That sounded a bit better. At least there was a plan.

"How soon can we do that?"

"I need another week," she said. "Can we wait that long?"

"As long as you need."

"How is your own practice going?"

"Fine," he lied. The truth was that he had been so concerned about her that he hadn't been able to do much of his own magic. It didn't seem to work very well without Amelia. But he didn't want to worry her with that.

"Let's go back," she said, tugging on his hand, and he resisted.

"Wait."

"For what?"

"For this."

He pulled her close and placed his lips on hers, melding them together as he gripped the back of her head and held her close. His lips moved on hers as he showed her, instead of telling her, all that he felt for her and how important she had become to him

## THE CURSED PORTRAIT

She responded in equal measure, and he found that the more emotion he put into the kiss, the more passion she returned.

Maybe this was it—this was the answer. Showing her how he felt drew her back to him.

One thing was for certain: He didn't want to let her go. He couldn't.

* * *

RELIEF WASHED over Amelia as she and Max walked back to the house together.

She was not alone in this.

He was there with her, every step of the way.

Amelia had lived most of her life alone. After her parents passed, she made her solitary way forward, supporting herself in a world that didn't make it easy for women.

She had always been proud of her ability to do so, and yet she found that it was a lot nicer than she would have thought to be able to lean on someone else.

Max could keep her solidly anchored, even as Isolde attempted to rock her off course.

Isolde had been pulling her under, a little more so every time Amelia sat down in front of her portrait. She had tried to deny the darkness that was washing over her, but it had become undeniable over the past few days. Eventually, she'd had no choice but to tell Max about it.

She had been nervous to do so, knowing he would react as he had, wanting her to leave the painting — which would mean leaving him.

Something she couldn't do.

They stopped outside the door of the music room, and Max grasped her by the shoulders.

"I'm going to stay with you."

"No," she argued. "You have so much else to do. You hired me to do this and I—"

"Do you truly think this is about what I have hired you to do any longer?" he asked, lifting a brow, making his handsome face even more attractive. "You have done more for me than anyone else in my life ever has, and I know that it is not because I am paying you to do so."

"You have a big heart," she said quietly. "You deserve everything you desire."

"I desire *you*," he said, and her breath caught at the passion in his voice. She had felt his passion before, but there was more to this now. They had been together physically, but she knew, deep within her, that he wasn't just talking about having her body. They were bound together in every way, and she felt it as much as he did.

"You have me," she whispered and kissed him again, drawing from him all of the light and power she needed to stay strong when she returned to the portrait.

She could do this.

All she needed was Max.

## CHAPTER 15

*You can help her, you know.*

Max rubbed his forehead as his grandfather's voice invaded. It was a week after Amelia had confessed Isolde's pull on her and Amelia said she had nearly finished Isolde's portrait. She had decided that the best way to stay true to herself was to take breaks from Isolde's painting and to work on her own. Whenever she finished for the day, Max could feel that she was refreshed, happier, calmer than she had been when she had been working only on Isolde's portrait.

*I am helping her. I'm there with her every step of the way.*

*You can do more.*

*How?*

*Protect her. Cast a spell around her to keep her safe.*

*I don't know how to do that.*

*You could if you tried. Do what you did before. Think of keeping her safe and infuse her with all of your power. It will create the spell you are looking for.*

Max remembered what Amelia had told him. To believe in himself.

He stood outside the music room, watching her work. He closed his eyes, held his arms out toward her, and did as his grandfather had said, sending her all of the protection he could infuse upon her.

His fingertips tingled before the power started to flow from them toward her. He watched in astonishment as a rainbow bubble began to form around her, and he could only hope that it would be enough to help keep her from Isolde's grasp.

Amelia didn't seem to notice as she continued her focus, and he sat watching her, wondering if he was imagining the ease in her brow or if she truly did seem more tranquil.

He could only hope he had helped her.

When he'd told her that he would do anything for her, it was the truth. If this came down to a sacrifice, he had to make sure that he was the one giving something away. Not her. She was more precious than anything else he owned or was a part of him – including his family name.

It had been such a short time, and yet, this woman had found a way into his heart. Now he just had to keep her safe.

\* \* \*

When Amelia finished her work that evening, she sat back, blinking at the portrait in front of her. She had done it. Isolde sat there, staring back at her, her expression all-knowing, bright and vivid now. Her hair was painted in the vermillion that Max had bought for Amelia, and she stared at her as though she could read all of Amelia's thoughts.

Maybe she could.

*I can.*

Amelia blinked. Had Isolde just spoken to her? She hadn't heard anything from her in all the time she had sat here in front of her. Why would she start now? Did it have to do with completing the painting?

*He doesn't love you. He is just using you.*

Amelia shook her head, trying to clear Isolde's voice from it. It was low, sultry, and she could see why she had cast such an intoxicating spell around Max's grandfather. She could understand why others had supposed that Isolde had spellbound Edward to her, but after feeling the depths of her pain, she knew that there had been genuine love there.

*Then he threw it all away.*

"He didn't," Amelia said, trying to convince her. "He loved you. His father tried to trick both of you. Edward was just as heartbroken as you were."

*Not heartbroken enough to stay true to me.*

"He married, yes, but it wasn't love. He loved *you*."

*Just as you think your Maximillian loves you.*

Amelia started, blinking at Isolde. "I never said that he loved me."

*But you want him to.*

She did. She knew it, deep within her heart. She was never one to shy away from emotion. It was what created the best artwork. When looking at a piece, she could always tell without even using her powers whether or not the artist had any care for the subject on the canvas.

But loving Max… it was a risk. One, however, she was willing to take.

*Don't. He will throw you away. You and I are not the type of women that these men are looking for. They use us for what we can offer them. Magic. Intimacy. And then they toss us away, even if they do feel affection for us.*

"That's not true," Amelia said stubbornly. "Max isn't like that."

Isolde's eyes were hypnotizing, trying to draw her in.

*You have power. True power. Together, we could be unstoppable. Just think of it.*

Amelia stood so fast that she tripped on the stool upon which she was sitting. Even as Isolde's painting tried to draw her in, she turned her head to look instead at the painting sitting beside it. It was the one she had been working on. It captured her and Max, an image of them in an embrace when they had first come together outside in the gardens.

She had painted the gardens as she had seen them, with the vegetation returning to its natural surroundings, encompassing them in their true form, instead of the haphazard unmanicured gardens that others might see them as. It was just as she saw the feelings they had together. She had infused in it all of the affection that she felt for him and all that she wished for their future.

Amelia looked away from it and back to Isolde. She closed her eyes, knowing where her heart was drawing her toward.

Isolde was wrong. What was between her and Max was enough. It had to be.

\* \* \*

"It's finished."

Max looked up from where he sat comfortably slouched in his chair at the dining table, waiting for Amelia.

She hadn't changed for dinner and was still wearing her paint-splotched apron over her morning dress.

"Isolde's portrait? Or your painting?"

"Both," she said, exhaustion lining her face and yet, there was still a bright glow to her expression, as though her energy was slowly returning. "We're ready."

He stood, walking over to her and wrapping his arms around her.

# THE CURSED PORTRAIT

"Thank you. For everything."

"There's nothing to thank me for," she said, leaning back and staring at him with such trust in her eyes that he nearly fell for her all over again. "Are you ready?"

"Of course," he said with more confidence than he actually felt. He knew that she could hold up her end of everything, but he wasn't entirely sure of his own abilities. "When do you want to try?"

"Do we have all we need?" she asked as he led her over to a chair and the footman brought in the first course, although Max noted that she barely touched it. In fact, she hadn't eaten much since she had become so involved with completing the painting. He recalled that she had initially thought it would take her months to complete and now she had done it in weeks instead.

"I have my grandfather's signet ring," he confirmed. "It has always been in my possession. I still need to find the locket. My grandfather gave it to Isolde. I had thought it might be in the lady of the house's suite, but it isn't there."

"It was Isolde's," she said, shaking her head, recalling Isolde wearing the locket in her vision. Would it have been buried with her or would Edward have kept it? She guessed the latter if he loved her as she thought he had. "I would suspect it would be among your grandfather's things."

"We can go look up on the third story," he said. "It is where all of my relatives' things are kept."

"That will be the last piece that we need," she said. "I can create a spell that should hopefully complement it, along with the portrait and your own abilities."

"And then?"

"As soon as we find it, we can go ahead. Tomorrow?"

"Whenever you want," he said, even though his heart raced at the thought. It wasn't the breaking of the curse that scared him. It was that it could be the end of whatever this was between them. Even if they did what they set out to do, at what cost would it bring them? And if Amelia did lose her abilities, would she resent him for the rest of her life?

He supposed that either way, he was going to find out soon.

They ate dinner in near silence. Well, he ate. She barely touched her food.

As soon as they finished, she stood up abruptly.

"Shall we go?"

"Very well," he said as he rubbed his breastbone. He didn't like how obsessed she had become about this, although he hoped that once it was finished, she would return to the woman he had met at his art exhibition.

He took her hand, interlacing their fingers as they walked up the stairs, over the faded carpet that covered the hardwood.

It was a long walk all the way up to the final level and by the time they reached it, she was breathing harder, pressed against his side as the stairwell became narrower the higher they climbed.

He pushed open the door, which creaked with its lack of use. The musty smell hit them as they walked in, and as Max lifted the candle to cast light around the room, the shadows of sheet-covered furniture resembled ghostly spirits.

"Over here," he said, walking the path by memory to where his grandfather's vanity lay. While Max had sold much of the furniture from their other homes when he had parted with them to try to pay off the family's debts, there were a few pieces that he had kept for their sentimental purposes. He had wondered what would happen to them if he were to soon follow in the way of his parents, but perhaps — *perhaps* — there would be another earl in the family line.

Would Amelia agree to stay with him? Could she see

# THE CURSED PORTRAIT

herself as a wife and, possibly, a mother? He supposed they would have to go through this ritual to find out first.

Amelia released his hand, walking across the room right toward the vanity as though she knew exactly where to go.

Before he could set the candle down and help her, she was lifting the sheet off of it and opening the top drawer.

She reached her hand in and pulled out what appeared to be the locket. The heart shaped pendant lay in her palm, the chain trailing off her hand beside it.

"It's here," she said, turning to him, and he nearly stepped back in shock as her eyes had taken on an other-worldly glow. "It's mine."

He crossed over to her, wrapping his hands around hers. "Amelia," he said urgently. "It is not yours. It is hers. Isolde's. You are not her. You are not tied together. Do you understand?"

Her green eyes flashed for a moment as though she was trying to come back to herself before she nodded. "Yes. Of course."

"Good," he said. "Remember that, all right?"

"Yes," she agreed, although it was with less confidence than he would have liked.

"Why don't I hold onto it?" he asked, sensing that she was having difficulty letting go of the locket.

He reached his hand out to take the piece of jewelry, and while she allowed the chain to sit in his palm, it took her a moment to actually release the pendant.

"Come," he said. "There is nothing more to do tonight. Let's go to bed."

She allowed him to lead her downstairs, and when they reached the landing, she leaned into him.

"I'm so tired," she whispered.

"I know," he said, placing a kiss on her temple. "Come along."

He led her down the corridor into the room, removing her painting apron before unfastening the ties on the back of her gown and slowly slipping it off her shoulders. He appreciated the soft skin of her upper arms, noted with a frown the way her collarbones were standing out even more so than usual, and thanked God that he was the one lucky enough to be tucking her into his bed clad only in her chemise.

Isolde and her curse were taking a toll on her. He vowed to put everything to rights and bring that smile back onto her face.

"Goodnight," he said, placing a kiss on her cheek. "Sleep well."

Her eyelids slowly fluttered closed, and as he stared down at her, his hand on hers, that sense of protection he had been searching so hard for came barreling out of him, the spell so forceful that it was a wonder it didn't wake her up.

But in that instant, Max knew.

This was the feeling, the spell that he had been waiting for.

Now he just had to figure out how to fight from within it to forces beyond.

Because they were never taking Amelia.

Never.

## CHAPTER 16

Max had been prepared for their plan to break the curse to go all wrong.

He had assumed a wide variety of reasons that might prevent it.

Perhaps Isolde would get angry and attack them supernaturally. Maybe he and Amelia would both lose all of their powers. Conceivably it could be called off by his own untimely death.

What he hadn't been prepared for was an onslaught of visitors, both noble and beyond.

It started with Lord and Lady Grantham, who called upon him the afternoon after he and Amelia had found the locket. They had been friends of his parents, but he had always found them rather pompous.

He recalled seeing them at his art exhibition. He had assumed they had attended simply to collect gossip, although Lady Grantham had made the excuse that she was keeping an eye on him on behalf of his mother.

When Whitaker announced them, Max wondered whether they would believe it if he said he wasn't in.

But it was far too obvious that he was in residence, so he reluctantly greeted them in Blackwood Manor's drawing room.

"Lord Blackwood, we apologize for imposing, but when we didn't receive a return letter, we knew we must come to call upon you as we passed by on our way to our own estate," Lady Grantham said effusively, even as her gaze wandered around the room with interest. Max wondered how much of this visit was due to her wanting to collect information about his current living situation.

"I apologize," he said stiltedly. "I have been busy."

"We are offering you a sizeable sum for the Roman statue of the young woman," Lord Grantham said. "It was one of your mother's favorites, and my wife would like it to remember her by. Would you be interested in accepting?"

Max pretended to be considering the offer, even though he was in disbelief. The timing might not be ideal, but was this actually going to turn out? He knew that Lord Grantham was, in part, making an excuse as this was a sought-after statue, but he was willing to play along.

"I am interested," he said, stroking his chin, "although it is a nearly priceless piece."

"I understand, my lord, but the moment I saw it again, I knew I had to have it," Lady Grantham said, even as her husband attempted to shush her, for she clearly didn't understand how bargaining worked. "May I see it again?"

"That could be arranged," Max said, needing this deal but hoping it could take place another day. "When could you return?"

"Actually, we were hoping to see it today," Lord Grantham said apologetically. "We will not be this way for some time again now, so we were hoping we could complete this before we left."

# THE CURSED PORTRAIT

"We could always stay over," Lady Grantham said hopefully, but Max was already shaking his head.

"No need. We can do this quickly."

They stood and he was just about to show them into the ballroom when Amelia came walking in, her head down. "Max, I—"

She stopped suddenly when she nearly walked right into Lady Grantham. Belatedly, she lifted her head and realized that they were not alone.

"Oh, goodness, I am so sorry. I didn't know you had company," she said, before slowly beginning to back out of the room.

"Oh, no problem whatsoever," Lady Grantham said, a wide, knowing smile on her face. "And who might this be?"

Amelia looked from her to Max and back again, but she most certainly wasn't the type of woman to back down, no matter who she was facing – even when she was wearing a faded painting apron over a rather worn morning gown. Max had seen her face Isolde without fear. He doubted she would back down from Lady Grantham.

"I am Amelia Lennox," she introduced herself, even though her eyes were wide and rather drawn from the long days and late nights she had been keeping. "The earl hired me to restore one of the portraits in his collection."

"The earl?" Lady Grantham said, her eyes flashing as she obviously hadn't missed Amelia calling him by his given name when she had first walked in the room.

"Yes," Amelia said slowly as though she was talking to a child. "Who else here would have hired me?"

"Of course," Lady Grantham said, slightly flustered, and Max had to hide his grin behind his hand. "Are you staying here?"

"There isn't anywhere else nearby, is there?" Amelia said, raising a brow in challenge.

"Of course not," Lady Grantham said. "Well, the servants' quarters here at Blackwood were always well kept up, if I remember correctly."

"I am sure they are," Amelia said, folding her hands in front of her, neither confirming nor denying her current accommodations.

"Lord and Lady Grantham are interested in possibly buying one of the statues in my collection. The Roman young lady," Max explained. "I am taking them to the ballroom to view it again."

"Lovely," Amelia said with a small smile. "It is a beautiful piece."

"I shall see you soon," Max said, resting a hand on her shoulder for longer than one would touch a friend – or most especially someone in his employ – as he walked by her. The truth was, he didn't care what these people, nor anyone else, thought of him and his relationship with Amelia. Let them talk. After everything they had faced so far, a little gossip amongst the *ton* meant absolutely nothing.

Amelia watched him with wide eyes as though understanding just what he was doing, and he winked at her as he led Lord and Lady Grantham out.

She needed to know that she came first.

Now and always.

\* \* \*

AMELIA HAD BEEN TAKEN ABACK when she had come upon the noble couple in the drawing room. She had been most excited to share with Max the incantation she had written that she was certain would break the curse, but that would have to wait. They certainly couldn't risk anything with others here.

Actually, come to think of it, they must make sure not to

anger Isolde today. It was one thing to cause gossip that an unattached, unchaperoned young woman was staying with the earl. Having an angry spirit involve them in her curse would be quite another.

Amelia was rounding the bottom of the grand staircase near the front foyer to return to her bedroom to prepare for the ritual when a knock sounded on the front door. She paused, a hand on the banister as she waited for Whitaker to answer it, but when she didn't hear footsteps approaching, she walked to the door and opened it herself.

She nearly fell over at the person who was standing on the other side.

"Charlie!" she gasped. "What are you doing here?"

"Is that any way to greet a travel-weary friend?" he asked with a chuckle as he held his arms out to her. She stepped into them woodenly, still in shock. "I came to make sure that you were well. You have been gone for a time with no word. I had to make sure that the earl hadn't trapped you in a tower where he was holding you as his prisoner."

She laughed slightly. "No chance of that," she said. "He has actually been a very welcoming host."

She wasn't about to tell Charlie just *how* welcoming he had been.

"This is not exactly close to London," she said, leading him into the house.

"You don't seem particularly happy to see me," he said with a frown, leaning in close – a bit too close for her liking. She had always known he had feelings for her, but now she didn't want to jeopardize the bond she and Max had formed.

"I am always happy to see you," she said truthfully. "It is just that this project does not provide me much time to myself. I do not want to see you here bored and lonely."

He laughed. "I am very rarely bored or lonely. That being said, I am actually staying with a friend in the area, so it was convenient for me to come by and see how you were. I will not be staying."

Relief swept through Amelia, startling her. She had always been one to welcome time spent with others. She considered her life in London, which was full of her society meetings, whether that be with her artist group or her magical one. It all seemed so far removed now, as she had become so caught up with her current purpose that she had nearly forgotten herself.

*It's his fault.*

She shook Isolde's voice out of her head. It was not Max's fault. He had hired her to do a job, and she was following through. It was Isolde's fault.

She sensed Isolde's frustration, and calmed her mind as she remembered that now was not the time to rile the spirit.

"Would you like to come in for tea?" she asked Charlie now, more brightness in her tone than she actually felt. But since Max was currently entertaining, she didn't see any harm in doing so herself. "I am sure that Lord Blackwood wouldn't mind, and his servants are most welcoming."

"I would love to," he said, following her deeper into the manor, his head craning around as he took in all of the pieces covering the walls, as well as the dark spaces where paintings had lived before they were sold. She remembered her own first foray around the house and imagined that he was noting all of the same things. Amelia detoured around the drawing room, not wanting to encounter Max and his guests, leading Charlie to the back parlor room. She encountered a maid along the way and asked her to advise the housekeeper where they were and to please bring tea.

As soon as the eager maid left, Charlie sank into a sofa and looked at Amelia piercingly, his expression more serious than she had ever seen it before.

"Are you sure you are well?" he asked. "You look rather... drawn."

"I'm fine," she insisted, needing him to believe her so that he wouldn't cause any additional turmoil. This house had enough of it already. "This has been a difficult job, but one I should complete in due time."

"When you are finished with it, what will you do?" he asked. "Will you return to London right away? We miss you there. I miss you. It's where you belong."

"I—" she opened her mouth to answer, but as she did, she saw motion in the door, and looked to see Max's figure striding away.

"Amelia?"

She returned her attention to Charlie.

"I am not certain of the future yet," she said with a forced smile. "Taking things one day at a time, as I always do. Now, tell me, how are you enjoying my former London accommodations?"

The change in subject distracted him, and they continued to chat about nothing of true consequence as the housekeeper herself brought the tea in. Finally, after an hour or so, Amelia began to get a bit twitchy.

Before she could say anything, Max appeared in the doorway as though he had sensed her unease.

"Amelia," he greeted her with a nod, "how is your day?"

"Just fine," she said. "My lord, I am not sure if you recall Charlie Bastian?" she gestured to her friend who was sitting across from her, now leaning forward with his elbows on his knees and a frown on his face as he scrutinized Max.

"Ah, yes, you were one of the artists invited to my exhibition," Max said. "Amelia told me that you secured another commission at the event."

"Yes, a portrait of Mr. and Mrs. Anderson," Charlie said proudly. "Already finished it and I am happy to say they were quite pleased with it. I was nearby visiting so I came to check in on Amelia. It has been some time since I had heard from her."

"It seems everyone was in the area today," Max murmured as Lord and Lady Grantham stepped into the room behind him, Lady Grantham looking awfully pleased with herself.

"Another visitor! Why, my lord, I didn't know you were so keen on hosting. Miss Lennox, I am delighted to find you are still here," Lady Grantham said, walking toward her. "I have so much to ask you. I have never had much talent myself besides the odd watercolors, but I do enjoy the art of others."

As she introduced herself to Charlie, expressed her delight to find that he was also an artist, and then launched into her questions about their careers, Amelia wondered whether she and Max would ever be able to continue with the day they had planned.

It seemed they were about to find out.

## CHAPTER 17

*M*ax was not enjoying any part of this situation.
He didn't like Charlie's familiarity with Amelia, although he was smart enough not to comment on it.

He wasn't pleased that Lord and Lady Grantham hadn't left after making their agreement as they said they were going to.

And he most certainly was annoyed at how Amelia looked like she was about to fall over. For such a vibrant woman, she had lost much of her brightness, and he was sure that Charlie had noted it, if the way he was looking between Max and Amelia was any sign. He most certainly seemed to suspect that Max was to blame.

The worst part of it was that Charlie was right. It was Max's fault.

The sooner he could get them all out of here, the sooner they could break this curse, be done with it, and hopefully restore Amelia's vitality.

But it was not as though he could share that with any of them.

However, dinner hour was nearing, and soon, he would

either have to invite them all to stay or send them on their way.

He knew which was the polite option. But he had no wish to do it.

"Where did you say you were staying, Charlie?" Amelia asked, clearly of the same mind as Max.

"With Lucas Albright," he said. "You remember him?"

"I do," she said. "He is a brilliant sculptor."

"He lives near here now," Charlie said. "He says he draws his inspiration from the countryside and finds the city far too cloying. He said it stifles his creativity."

"How lovely that you could see him," she said with a warm smile, and Max was reminded of how well she fit with other people – unlike him and this mausoleum he had forced her into. "I shall have to arrange a visit before I leave."

"I would love to see you again," Charlie said, leaning in close and placing a hand on Amelia's arm for long enough that Max wanted to growl at him to remove it. "Perhaps you can do so while I am still here."

"I will do my very best," she said, and Charlie looked over at Max.

"I hope you are not working her too hard, my lord."

He said it in jest, but Max was aware that there was an underlying current of warning beneath it.

"I have found that Miss Lennox is the one who insists on working herself too hard," Max said. "I would actually prefer that she rest more."

"I am glad we are in agreement," Charlie said. "As you are the one here with her, you will have to be sure to remind her."

Max only lifted an eyebrow.

While Charlie might be correct, he was an artist, and Max was an earl. He wasn't used to being spoken to as such, and it seemed that Charlie quickly realized it as he hastily covered his mistake.

"Which I am sure you do. You seem a most gracious employer."

"My lord is the best of *gentle*men," Lady Grantham said enthusiastically, although her eyes were sharp as she was clearly understanding some of the tensions that lined the room.

Max sighed and rubbed the bridge of his nose as he saw Whitaker lingering in the doorway, likely wondering about the approaching dinner hour.

"Lord and Lady Grantham. Mr. Bastian, would you like to st—" He hadn't even gotten the word out when there was a rumbling from beyond. He looked through the parlor window but found that the skies were clear. If there wasn't any thunder, that meant—oh bollocks. It seemed Isolde wasn't interested in hosting guests tonight.

"What was that?" Lady Grantham asked, looking around.

"Perhaps someone was moving something elsewhere in the manor," Amelia said helpfully, even as her eyes met Max's in concern.

"It could be," he said. "We are doing something of a... renovation. That is part of why Miss Lennox is here working on one of my most prized paintings."

"I see," Lady Grantham said, her eyes flicking back and forth between them as she was obviously quite interested in this lie they were concocting, although Max couldn't be sure what she actually believed. "Could we see the work you are doing?"

"It is too dangerous," Max said. "Scaffolds, high bricks... I would not want anyone to be hurt."

"Where in the manor is—"

A door suddenly slammed down the hallway, followed by

a succession of more slams that echoed one another, each farther away.

"My goodness," Lady Grantham said, bringing a hand to cover her mouth. "I recall your mother saying that this place was haunted, but I always thought that she just had an overactive mind. I never believed in such nonsense myself. But..." she looked around thoughtfully. "This all seems rather strange."

Her husband, a silent man, was already standing near the door, fists clasped in front of him.

"I believe the Crawleys are expecting us, dear," he said. "We best go."

His face was drawn in fear. Apparently, as much as Lady Grantham didn't believe in hauntings, her husband did.

Isolde's plan had worked.

*She always was a smart one.*

*Are you still interested, then, Grandfather?*

*She cursed our family.*

Max sighed. So much for that idea. He had hoped that if he could get his grandfather to forgive Isolde, they might be able to rediscover the love that the curse had discussed.

But his grandfather was a stubborn one, even though Max sensed that, deep within, he still held love for Isolde.

Max recognized the emotion himself.

He stood to walk Lord and Lady Grantham to the front door, although he couldn't help but overhear Charlie's conversation with Amelia.

"I suppose that is my cue to leave as well," he said, "although I do not like leaving you here alone."

"Charlie," she said with a slight chuckle. "I am not alone. The earl is in residence, as are his staff. I can assure you that I will be perfectly fine."

Charlie lowered his voice slightly, but Max could still

hear him. "Something isn't right here, Amelia. I can feel it, deep in my bones."

"Just some lonely spirits," she said flippantly. "Nothing to be concerned about."

As Charlie had not been invited to stay, he certainly couldn't say anymore, but Max did try to stay close enough that he could prevent any additional line of questioning.

Lord and Lady Grantham were out the door so quickly he barely had time to say farewell and thank them for stopping by before the door slammed behind them. He turned to find Charlie standing there, looking around apprehensively.

"Amelia," he said slowly, "why do you not come stay with me and Lucas for the night? He would love to see you, and it isn't far. You could return here to work during the day. Actually, yes, I think that would be far preferable—"

Max fisted his hands as he tried to tamp down the ire that was growing inside of him, and he stepped forward menacingly. "Amelia—" He was about to say rather forcefully that she was staying *here*. That this was where she belonged. That she was his, and she would not be going anywhere that required her sleeping in the home of a man who wasn't him.

But then he remembered everything that Amelia had told him. How proud she was that she had made her way in the world by herself, without a man looking after her. That she spoke for herself and only for herself. And he knew then that if he said what he was truly feeling, he would only push her away.

He took a breath to calm himself, cleared his throat, and tried again. "Amelia has the ability to make her own decisions. I think it would be better if you *asked* her rather than told her."

He looked back at her, desperately hoping that she would decline.

She was staring at him with amazement in her face. Then her lips curled up in a small smile.

"Thank you," she said softly before turning to Charlie. "I appreciate the offer, Charlie, and I will come to visit sometime soon. But I shall stay here."

Max waited for her to say that she was waiting until she finished the work, or that she would be returning to London in due time, but she left it where it was, and he had to wonder what that meant.

Charlie nodded, obviously wanting to say more but knowing it was not his place to do so before he said goodnight and walked out the door.

After Isolde slammed it behind him, Amelia looked at Max expectantly. There was so much to say, so much that they needed to do.

But first, he needed to kiss her with the same intensity that he needed to breathe.

He wrapped her in his embrace, loving how she felt in his arms, which was exactly where she belonged. He leaned her over, dipping her backward as he kissed her soundly, reveling in the sensual response of her lips actively seeking him out as she reached up and held him against her.

Their kiss was a symphony of emotions and unspoken words. As his lips moved over hers, a surge of electricity coursed through Max, igniting the embers of emotion that had been smoldering deep within his heart. Her taste was intoxicating, and he couldn't help but deepen the kiss, losing himself in the moment.

Amelia's hands tangled in his hair, pulling him closer as if afraid he might vanish if she let go. Her touch was gentle yet fervent, a silent plea for him to stay close. Max could feel the raw passion emanating from her, matching his own desire with a fierce intensity that took his breath away.

## THE CURSED PORTRAIT

Finally, she leaned back, gasping for breath as her eyes met his in a soul-searching moment.

"Max," she whispered. "I…I…"

He waited with bated breath. Did she love him? Could she? Did he want her to say the words?

Yes, he did – with all his heart. No one had ever chosen him before, nor even appeared to want him for any reason other than that he was a powerful earl. Even his parents had not been around long enough to convince him that he was worth the love of another.

Suddenly a mask flashed over her eyes, and he lost her for just a moment.

"What is it?" he asked. "What's wrong?"

She stepped back, her arms falling away from him and down to her sides.

"She's calling me," she murmured, the glaze covering her eyes. "She wants… she wants *me*."

She began to step backward toward the door as panic beat deep within Max's chest. He reached out, following Amelia, catching her hands and holding them against his chest.

"I'm here," he said urgently. "Fight it. Fight her. I am with you. Stay, Amelia. Please."

His voice had grown to a shout as he tried to hold on, and she shook her head violently as she was obviously trying to fight Isolde out of her mind.

"Max," she cried out. "We have to break this. Now. If she takes me over… I don't… I don't know if I can come back from it. It's like a darkness sucking me in. But a tempting darkness that's getting harder to resist."

Max cried out a curse before bending down and scooping her into his arms. Damn their visitors from today. If they hadn't had to pause, they could have been done with this hours ago. Instead, both he and Amelia were now tired and hungry and had to break a curse cast by a sorceress who appeared to be growing ever more powerful by the moment.

Seeing he was losing Amelia, Max carried her downstairs to the music room, knowing that he was going to have to finish a lot of the work that Amelia had started. He could do this. He had to.

He laid Amelia down on the sofa that lined the side of the room. She was still there in body, but her eyes had taken on an eerie glow. Max lined up facing Isolde's portrait, which was now practically gleaming in the light that was streaming in through the window, light that he realized was lightning, streaking through the sky.

It seemed that Isolde was aware of what they were planning to do and had decided to begin her own onslaught.

Max closed his eyes, trying to remember the incantations and symbols that Amelia had discovered through the painting and she thought they needed to break the curse, but found he couldn't remember them properly. She had also been working on the right incantation but hadn't had a chance to share it with him.

Why hadn't he paid more attention to her?

He knelt beside her, placing his hands on her shoulders and looking deeply into her eyes.

"Amelia," he said, trying to speak to her soul instead of her mind. "I need you with me now. I need your help. We have to break this curse, and we have to break it now."

She blinked a few times, the sheen lessening somewhat each time before her eyes cleared slightly and she stared back at him.

"Yes. Yes. I'm here."

"Good," he said in relief, reaching out and wrapping his arm around her head before placing a kiss against her forehead. "Let's do this."

## CHAPTER 18

Amelia's head spun as she tried to recall all of the knowledge she had acquired to break the curse, punctuated by Isolde's constant insistence that she was not meant for this.

*You will never be a countess. You are an artist from a poor family. He is using you to be rid of me. I was where you were, thinking I was special, but the family threw me away. Do not allow the same to happen to you. Together, we can be so much more.*

Deep in her soul, Amelia knew that Isolde was trying to manipulate her, but the power she was sending toward her, which was now coursing through her veins, was so tempting that it was hard to deny her.

Looking at Max, however, she knew he was where her true future lay – in whatever form it would end up taking. Isolde used magic and illusion to try to convince Amelia of the way forward. Max was simply his true self and had given her everything she had ever asked of him and more. She had to believe in that and in him.

Together, they could fight Isolde's power.

She took a breath. "Max, could you start by creating

protection around us? It might not hold, but it should help shield us some from whatever Isolde tries to send our way."

"I shall do my best," he said, standing back, his face opening up to the world around him as his arms stretched out wide. "Fire, water, earth, air," he murmured, seemingly gathering all of it in his arms as the room began to swirl with wind, flame, liquid, and soil. Amelia's mouth dropped open as all of the elements began to answer his call, swimming around them. Finally, they all bonded together, forming a circle of protection and power around the two of them.

When Max opened his eyes, he seemed just as shocked as Amelia at what he had accomplished, as a purplish glow hovered in the air around them in a circle.

"I did it," he said in astonishment.

"You did," she said, awestruck. She had been falling for him before, but now, with this new vulnerability about him, she knew that theirs was a bond that could never be broken. She believed in it as much as she believed in all of the strength that surrounded them.

"I have the incantation ready," she said, reaching into her pocket to find the words she had written, that she had wanted to share with Max earlier but didn't have the chance thanks to their visitors. "First, you need to call upon your ancestors for their guidance and strength. This will help to stabilize our ritual and bring all of the true memories to light."

"Do you think that will anger Isolde?"

"She remembers only the worst of it all. Everyone has their own version of the truth, but perhaps we can piece together what actually happened with shared memories."

"You can do that? Bring them all together?" he asked, shocked, and she felt her first dip in confidence.

"I can try."

He had never done it before, but there was no better time than this moment.

"Very well," he said before he took a breath and called to his ancestors out loud.

"Grandfather. And whoever else might be listening. I need your help. We must break this curse and keep our family alive. Be with us. Help us. Show us what we need."

He closed his eyes as he seemed to hear a response, but before he could share it with Amelia, a piercing scream resounded within the room. Amelia screwed her eyes closed as she covered her ears with her hands, trying to prevent Isolde's anger from coursing through her own body.

"She doesn't want them here," Amelia cried out, but Max took her hands and clenched them tightly.

"They're here anyway," he said, and they looked around them in shock as the spirits had manifested in near-physical form, practically floating around the room. They all appeared as they did in their portraits, and when Amelia looked at the portrait she had worked on for weeks now, she was shocked to find that Isolde was no longer within it, but had floated outside of it, the colors of her gown the only thing that was still attaching her to the canvas. She was trying to reach them, to reach Amelia, but it appeared that Max's protective shield had worked and was keeping her out, although the purplish red glow seemed to flicker and dim every time Isolde surged toward them.

Max reached into his own pocket, pulling out the locket that Isolde had desired to possess ever since Amelia had discovered it. She felt her own pull toward it and wondered whether it was wise for Max to give it to her. He obviously had the same concern, for he paused momentarily before handing it over to Amelia.

Amelia hesitated as she wasn't sure she would have enough power to resist, but she knew she had to trust herself. She grasped the locket in her hands and fastened the clasp around her neck. It pulsed with the eerie green light as she closed her eyes, trying to resist its intoxicating pull.

It was calling to her, threatening to draw her in and under, but then Max pulled out the signet ring that matched it and slid it onto his finger.

Amelia drew a huge intake of breath as a new kind of power surged through her. Max's ring was not only part of the spell – it centered her, steadying the power of her locket and tying the two of them together.

"This can be yours, Isolde," Amelia said, lifting the locket toward her. "I just need you to agree to stop fighting this – stop fighting us."

The wind in the room began whipping around them, indicating that Isolde's response was far from favorable.

A clanging came from beyond the room, and Amelia whipped her head toward the doorway to see what new threat could be emerging, her breath catching in her throat at the shield and swords dancing down the corridor, animated as though they were living beings.

"Bloody hell!" Max exclaimed as he swiped a hand through his hair before pushing Amelia behind him. They were still within the protective bubble, but the swords hurled themselves toward them, each one getting closer to piercing their surrounding shield.

"We need to do something!" Max shouted, and Amelia reached out, grabbing his hand to ground herself.

"Isolde," she shouted. "You need to reconcile the past. We need to learn what happened to find the love that remains. I know it's there. I know you can find it within yourself. Within Edward."

She closed her eyes, reaching deep into the memories that Isolde had shared from the painting, using Max's power through their joined hands and spirits to reach his ancestors and find the answers from them.

She took the shared memories, combining them together as she tried to assemble the truth.

She could sense shouting in the room around her from both Max and the other spirits that had invaded the music room, but she had to leave that be and trust that Max could protect her while she crafted this within her head.

Finally, when she had everything formed as properly as she could, she opened her eyes and launched the truth into the air, allowing them all to see for themselves just what had happened.

In the air above them was cast the same scene that Isolde had shown her before, but this time, there was a new perspective – that of Max's grandfather. Edward stood at the door, distraught, as he learned that the lies of his father had led to the loss of the love of his life.

"How could you?" he shouted. "I love her!"

"It is too late," his father said, as Isolde lay collapsed on the ground before him. "She is gone. When I told her that you no longer wanted her, her hatred for you grew and she has no wish to be near you anymore. Find another, Edward. One who will match you in every way possible."

"I don't care who she is or where she is from. *She* is the one that I want."

"She bewitched you."

"She did nothing of the sort."

The two men engaged in a battle of wills until both of them were rocked apart by an explosion that ripped through the entirety of Blackwood Manor.

Isolde's curse, the surviving part of her, wove around them in an eerie green glow, completely encompassing them until their souls were dyed with it.

"What is happening?" Edward whispered before they

were launched back to Isolde's perspective – only instead of her physical form, she had become her spirit, her pain overtaking her and fueling her entire being. All of her power had seeped into the curse she had cast as she sank into the painting, which completely consumed her as well as the spell itself.

Suddenly a roar split the air as one of the swords pierced through the bubble and into Max.

Amelia was launched back into the moment as Max's pain invaded her body, and the images above them faded away as she could no longer maintain her focus.

"Max!" she cried as she fell on top of him, sensing him throwing up his arms in an attempt to hold onto the protective spell as Amelia ripped off a piece of her dress and held it to his shoulder, trying to staunch the blood that poured through the wound.

"You have to go, Amelia," he cried. "She's not listening, and I cannot allow you to be hurt in the process."

"We're not done yet," she said, pushing herself up and off of him. As much as she wanted to stay and see to Max, she knew that if she didn't end this now, there would be no coming back from this for either of them.

She practically crawled across the room until she grasped the artwork that she had painted earlier – not Isolde's portrait, but the one of her and Max, caught together in the gardens. She held it up above her head as she began to speak the incantation she had written down, reciting it from memory.

*By the light of the moon and the stars that gleam,*
*I call upon forces seen and unseen.*
*What was wronged, now set to right,*
*Release this soul from endless night.*
*Through blood and time, the ties unbind,*
*No more shall shadows cloud this mind.*

# THE CURSED PORTRAIT

*By earth's deep roots and winds that sigh,*
*By flames that burn and seas that cry.*
*From ancient grief and sorrows deep,*
*I call forth peace, in love's name keep.*
*Let the curse that binds now fade away,*
*Bring forth the dawn, a brand new day.*
*With heart and will, by magic's key,*
*I break these chains, so mote it be.*

As she said the words, the image of her and Max entwined in an embrace swirled out of the portrait in a kaleidoscope of color, and she sent all of the love she felt for Max into the spell she cast.

Max called to the elements, binding them into the incantation, until they were all together to produce a spell more powerful than any Amelia had ever felt before.

She tried to send it all toward Isolde's portrait, where she knew the curse was held. She could only hope that Max's ancestors were providing their own power to help bind it all together.

Power radiated from her fingers, into the locket around her neck, until she felt it lifting off of her, reaching toward the portrait.

The colors that had painted her and Max together began to mix and swirl, until she nearly couldn't make out their forms anymore. With a crack in the air, the locket shot toward the portrait, and as Max's protection spell began to wane and the swords threatened to collapse right through it, Amelia reached deep within herself and sent every ounce of power she had into the spell.

She could feel Isolde's own anguish over all that had happened, and Amelia nearly thought all had been lost, that Isolde had become too powerful. Then Edward's spirit stepped forward, his voice raised to be heard over the magic that had overtaken the room.

"Isolde!" he cried. "Isolde, I never left you. You must believe how much I always loved you. How much I still want you now. I'm sorry for what happened. Truly I am. You were treated wrongly, but my family shouldn't have to suffer for my father's sins or my own stupidity."

While unsure whether Edward's words were true or whether he was trying to diffuse Isolde, Amelia felt Isolde's anger waver as she tried to decide whether or not to lessen the curse that surrounded them. The problem was, Amelia sensed then that the curse had become so powerful that it was now an entity within itself.

Isolde could break her ties with it, but unless Max and Amelia could counteract Isolde's spell, it would live on.

"Isolde, I will do all within my power to make things right," Max shouted toward her. "Take what you'd like, do what you want, just leave Amelia be. Do not make her suffer for my family's sins."

Amelia held Max's hand even tighter as her stare searched his while the weapons threatened ever closer. She had no idea whether the two of them would get out of this, but it was worth it all if she was going to be with him at this last moment.

"Max," she said, tears streaming from her eyes as she watched his own resolve turn to desperation. "Max, I love you."

As their lips fused together, the air charged with electricity, and a bang echoed throughout the music room.

Then everything went black.

## CHAPTER 19

The silence was deafening.

Max hadn't realized just how loud all the shouting was, nor the wind that had whipped through the room. The ground that had trembled beneath them and the flames that had roared in the fireplace were now still. Silent.

Amelia was limp in his arms, just barely breathing. He needed to see to her, to see to himself as blood continued to seep out of his wound, but first, he had to make sure that the danger had passed.

He blinked as he saw that most of his ancestors had vanished. His great-grandfather, who had simply watched disapprovingly, was fading back into his portrait, while all that remained was Edward and Isolde. Her vibrancy had faded, but her image stilled in the middle of the room until Edward's surged toward her, holding out a hand.

"Isolde," Edward said in a low voice, reaching to her. "Come with me. Forgive me."

She appeared to hesitate before she began to slide toward him, and finally, she reached out and clasped her hand with his before their spirits swirled together and faded back into Edward's painting – together.

Max blinked as he looked around the room, realizing that it was done.

It was over.

Whatever Amelia had done, whatever she had taken, had broken the curse. Isolde's portrait, now empty of its subject, began to crumble suddenly, disintegrating into the floor before them.

Max tried to lift Amelia, grunting when doing so strained his shoulder.

He staved away the pain before he lifted her in his arms, painstakingly carrying her out of this cursed music room. He climbed the stairs slowly but surely, aware that some of his staff had emerged and were staring at him, mouths agape. Why hadn't they all left? He was sure that this was going to be the end of any reputation he'd ever had – if he survived this.

Not that he particularly cared about that. All he cared about was making sure that Amelia was safe.

He finally reached his chamber and laid her down on the bed, beneath the beautiful mural she had magically painted when they had first come together.

"Amelia," he murmured. "Amelia, come back to me."

He ran his hand over her face, pushing away the wisps of hair that now framed it.

He would give anything for those beautiful blue-green eyes to open to him again and show him all of the love that he had been feeling between them, love that she had put into words.

"Amelia, I love you too," he said, bending down and pressing a soft kiss against her lips.

He closed his eyes and leaned his forehead against hers. This was what he had been afraid of – that in her quest to help him, she would lose herself and everything she held dear. Her powers, her vibrancy – her life.

He looked up toward the ceiling, the voices of his ancestors silent now at the time when he needed them the most.

"Why?" he cried out. "Why her? Why now? She did nothing but try to help us. To help me. The rest is worth nothing without her. How do I save her? All of her?"

He cried out a curse when he was met with silence. After everything they had been through, all he needed was for Amelia to be safe. Healthy. Happy. Whether that was with or without him, he no longer cared. But she shouldn't have to sacrifice for his family's curse to be broken.

Max didn't even know who he was supposed to call to help him. This wasn't a physical ailment but some type of magical suffering. If only he knew someone with powers he could ask for help, but he knew no one but those within his own family and Amelia herself.

He rested his head on her chest, allowing his tears to flow. "Please, Amelia," he whispered. "Please come back to me."

"Max?"

Her voice was weak, not much more than a murmur, but it was present. He lifted his head, meeting her eyes.

"Amelia?" he said urgently yet softly. "Amelia, are you there?"

"I'm not sure where else I would be," she said, the slightest bit of laughter in her voice.

"My God, I thought you were gone," he said, casting his head forward as relief coursed through him.

"You will not be rid of me that easily."

He cupped her face in his hands, pressing a soft kiss on her lips.

"You did too much," he said, running his hands along her soft skin.

"I did what was needed."

"But at what cost?" he asked, searching her eyes. "Do you still have your powers?"

"I'm not sure," she said, furrowing her brow. "I do not sense them as I once did. But perhaps they are just... resting. Even if they are gone, however, if we broke the curse, then it is worth it."

"Is it, though?" he asked, peering at her. "I never wanted anything to happen to you. You didn't deserve any fallout from this."

"It doesn't matter what I deserve or don't deserve," she said. "You didn't take it from me. I gave it. For you."

"Amelia," he said, needing her to know the full extent of his emotions. "I—"

"Max!" she cried out, her notice awakening more than anything else had as of yet. "You are bleeding."

"It's fine," he brushed it off. "It's just a scratch."

"That's more than a scratch," she insisted as she tried to sit up. "Let me see to it."

"You are barely coherent," he said. "Just sit for a moment. We need to rest."

There was a slight knock on the door before Mrs. Bloom called out. "My lord? Miss Lennox? Is there anything we can do?"

"Come in, Mrs. Bloom," Max called out, and she entered, a very worried expression on her face.

"My goodness, but you gave us a scare," she said. "We didn't know what to do. All of the shouting and wind and the rumbling had us nearly running from the manor."

"You *should* have left," Max said, shaking his head. "I never wanted any of you to be in danger."

"We would never leave you, my lord. Not after you refused to leave Blackwood and all that your family left you."

He blinked, the enormity of what she was saying sinking into him. He had thought that he was alone in the world, but

THE CURSED PORTRAIT

these people had chosen him. Servants, who could have left and found another job as easily as anything else. But why him?

"Because you are just as loyal as they are," Amelia said softly, reading his thoughts. "You are worthy of all love, Max."

He nodded stiffly as Mrs. Bloom assessed the situation and left, returning shortly with a basin full of fresh water, linen, and Max's valet. Together, they managed to clean and wrap the wounds, set all to rights, and soon a maid appeared with a tray. Max hadn't thought he was particularly hungry, but apparently, casting spells took a lot out of a person as he and Amelia both emptied the plate.

They looked at one another, words not necessary to say what they were both feeling – an intense, physical bond as well as one that went deeper than that, their souls interconnected in ways that he wouldn't have thought possible.

But now was not the time to discover that any further.

They were both exhausted and needed sleep to heal and recover.

The rest would just have to wait.

\* \* \*

AMELIA WOKE the next morning with her head on Max's chest – exactly where it belonged.

"Are you all right?" he asked, and she nodded lazily.

"I am. And you?"

"We are here together," he said, wincing as he pushed himself up into a sitting position, holding her close against him. "That is all that matters."

A maid arrived to help Amelia to her room to prepare for the day, and Max reluctantly released her, calling after her that he already missed her when she walked out the door.

Amelia smiled as she donned her gown, a lightness overcoming her that she hadn't felt in some time – and it wasn't only due to the lifting of the curse and the hold that Isolde had placed over her.

It was that she finally felt like she had found home. Not necessarily at Blackwood Manor, but with Max himself.

After they reunited and ate breakfast, Max asked if she would like to walk in the gardens. Amelia happily joined him, lifting her face to the sun when they met the walking path.

"I've never seen a woman so openly welcome the freckles onto her face," he remarked, and she fixed him with a curious gaze.

"Is that a criticism?"

"Not at all. I like to see the freedom you provide yourself." He stopped walking when they neared where the path turned into the forest beyond. "Have you tested your powers?"

She was silent momentarily, unsure of how much to tell him, for she didn't want him to blame himself.

"I have," she said slowly.

"And?"

"They do not appear to be active," she said. "But that doesn't mean they are gone. I am holding out hope. And you?"

His face had fallen at her news, but she hoped she could distract him from it. She was disappointed herself, having lost part of who she was and what she could do. She had been truthful when she had told Max, however, that it had been worth it. He didn't necessarily fill the void where her powers had been, but he added more to her life, a piece that she hadn't even known she had been missing.

"I haven't tried," he said, shaking his head, and she nodded toward a rock across the path.

"Try it now," she said, knowing that he would understand she was referring to the first time he had tested his abilities.

He looked at her skeptically but didn't deny her as he focused his attention on the rock.

Nothing happened.

"Try again," she urged, grabbing his hand, and only then did the rock give a little shake.

Was it her touch that had helped? Even if she didn't have her own powers... could she fuel his?

"I wonder..." she murmured, looking at him, wondering if he was feeling what she was thinking.

"Try again," she said, this time focusing all of her attention into his ability to move the rock. He nodded and she cried out in glee when the rock lifted and moved across the path.

"Now take my hands and infuse your power into me," she said, grabbing his hands before he could do anything. He seemed confused but agreed, and she closed her eyes and focused on the path in front of her.

There was a chance this could work. She told herself not to be disappointed if it didn't, but...

Rainbow blooms shot out where she had imagined them to be.

"That's it!" she exclaimed, nearly giddy with excitement. "Max, do you see what this means? My powers are not gone."

"They're not?"

"No!" she cried. "Ours are tied to each other. We need one another in order to make them work. Instead of losing our powers... we combined them."

She stared at him in awe. It didn't make sense, but did anything anymore? They were here together, and that was what mattered.

Max stepped toward her, taking her hands and folding them between them, his gaze intense upon her.

"Amelia," he said, his voice low, sincere, gravelly. "I need you to know that what I feel for you has nothing to do with magical powers. What I feel for you has no magic attached, no illusions. Just pure love. I don't care if we never use or have our powers again."

"You'd probably prefer that," she said with a laugh, and he chuckled.

"It is part of me now, and I am open to that. But my heart is yours, now and forever."

"And mine yours," she said, unable to stop the smile that bloomed from her lips.

"I know that you need people," he said. "Would you be happy spending time both here at Blackwood as well as in London?"

"Of course," she answered. "Wherever you are."

"We will make it work so that we will both be happy," he said. "I promise you that."

"I am happy with you," she said, lifting a hand and cupping his cheek.

"I love you, Amelia," he said.

"And I you."

When he leaned down and took her lips with his, he barely noticed the rainbow of color that escaped around them, nor the earth shaking beneath them.

All he discerned was Amelia herself, who was bound to him now and forever.

# EPILOGUE

*Amelia* and Max's entwined hands swung together as they walked through the halls of Blackwood Manor.

They had just returned from London, where they had married in front of the few from the *ton* that Max could suffer, as well as Amelia's friends, both magical and artistic.

To say that there had been a few raised eyebrows was an understatement, but neither of them cared. Max told her that after facing a curse and a scorned witch, the opinions of the *ton* were nothing.

"I hope Charlie was not too disappointed in our marriage," Max said to her now as though reading her mind – which, often it seemed, appeared to be connected to his.

"Perhaps at first, but I think he soon realized that he and I were not to be, that we will always be friends, but nothing more," Amelia said. "Actually, at our wedding, he met one of my friends from my *other* committee. A woman who seemed vaguely familiar to him. That should be an interesting pairing."

She grinned, and Max wondered what she had done to encourage the coupling.

"It certainly shall."

They stopped at the entrance to the ballroom, and Max met her gaze.

"Are you ready?"

"I am. And you?"

He nodded as they entered the ballroom-turned-art-gallery, slowly making their way along the number of family portraits that lined the wall. Amelia turned her nose up at Max's great-grandfather, her heart beating faster until they stood in front of Max's grandfather's portrait.

The one he now shared.

Amelia's breath caught in her throat at the image before her.

Edward remained, and while he was dressed in the same clothes as he had always been, he was no longer alone.

Unlike most portraits that would have been painted of couples in the previous century, they were not properly posed.

They were locked in an embrace, in the very same way that Amelia had painted herself and Max. Isolde's fiery hair flew out behind her, while Edward gazed at her with a hunger that Amelia well recognized from Max.

"I'm glad to see that Edward overcame his anger towards Isolde," Max murmured.

"I think it was all such a misunderstanding," Amelia said, looking up to him. "They did truly love each other. They just allowed so much pain to get in the way of it all."

"I agree," he said, turning his attention away from the portrait and toward Amelia. "Thank you for everything that you did for my family. For me. For helping us all see clearly, to appreciate the truth, and to be willing to give so much of yourself. It is hard to believe that the curse is finally broken."

"Every bit of it was worth it," she said. "I would do anything for you."

"And I you," he said. "I'm a very lucky man."

As he took her in his arms, music began to play from elsewhere in the manor. They had no idea if it was Isolde, or another spirit that had taken up residence, but Amelia knew that it no longer mattered. Max had welcomed it all. Had welcomed her.

And she had found her forever home.

"Max?"

"Yes?"

"I have something for you."

He lifted a brow as he waited, and she crossed the room to where Whitaker was waiting with her gift.

She lifted it in her arms and held it toward him. He couldn't help the grin that spread over his face. For there was the painting she had created of the two of them – the one she had used to break the spell.

"I told you that I wanted to paint you – and I am still going to have you pose for me." Her lips widened in a smile as she pictured just how she would pose him. "But I loved this one of us together. I thought we could put it here," she said. "Beside Isolde and Edward. What do you think?"

"It's perfect," he said, his smile now warm and sincere. "Forever together."

"Forever entwined," she declared. "As it should be."

\* \* \*

Dear reader,

I hope you enjoyed Max and Amelia's story! *The Cursed Portrait* combines my love of Regency, paranormal, and gothic romance. Would you like to read more stories like this? Let me know! Please email me at ellie@elliestclair.com, post in my facebook group or, of course, leave a review.

If you love gothic romance, keep reading for a preview of

Always Your Love, a standalone beauty-and-the-beast, arranged marriage Regency romance.

If you haven't yet signed up for my newsletter, I would love to have you join us! You will receive a free book as well as links to giveaways, sales, new releases, and stories about my coffee addiction, my struggle to keep my plants alive, and how much trouble one loveable wolf-lookalike dog can get into.

www.elliestclair.com/ellies-newsletter

Or you can join my Facebook group, Ellie St. Clair's Ever Afters, and stay in touch daily.

Until next time, happy reading!

With love,

*Ellie*

*Always Your Love*

**A scarred soldier. A dutiful daughter. An arranged marriage in an empty house with its own stories to tell.**

Lady Hannah Blackburn has always been an obedient daughter, doing exactly as she is told. So when her sister runs off with a footman and her parents decide on a hastily arranged marriage for her, she agrees. But when she kisses a stranger in the library on the same night her fiancée has a tryst of his own, everything changes.

Lord Edmund Marshville, a former soldier and the second son of an earl, has one desire — to be left alone with his scars and his memories in his remote Hollingswood Estate. When he gives in to his mother's plea to attend his brother's engagement party, he doesn't realize how life altering one night can be.

When Hannah and Edmund return to Hollingswood after their arranged marriage, it doesn't seem like they will ever be connected in anything more than name, until they begin to uncover secrets hidden for decades. Will attempting to reunite lost loves help them find their way to each other, or do the fates have other plans for them?

# AN EXCERPT FROM ALWAYS YOUR LOVE

*Hannah* Blackburn needed a moment.

A moment alone. A moment away from the crush of people. A moment away from Byron.

She took a shaky breath, closing her eyes as she pressed her hand against her throat and leaned against the back of the door.

As she began to restore her equilibrium, she opened her eyes, and allowed her gaze to wander over the shadows among the bookshelves, created by the dwindling flame in the fireplace at the far end of the room. It seemed she had stumbled upon a library. It had been the first door she had tried. The room was so full it was near bursting, with not only the expected books but also statues, vases, portraits, and unused frames littering the space.

A chesterfield sat in front of the fire, and Hannah took a step forward, drawn toward the warmth and comfort.

"What are you doing in here?"

Hannah jumped, whirling around to determine the voice's origin. Her heart pounded within her chest, but she was proud she hadn't emitted even the slightest of sounds.

"Who's there?" she demanded, though there was a break in her tone.

"Did I frighten you?" His voice was dry, containing a hint of sarcasm, although Hannah didn't see what could possibly be amusing about his words.

"You startled me," she said, peering into the shadows, finally making out his silhouette in the corner, sitting in an armchair that had been pushed back against the wall. "I'm sorry to have disturbed you," she said, thrown slightly off balance by the stranger who didn't seem to have any desire to make his identity known. "I'll leave you now."

"Don't go." The command he issued somehow contained a hint of pleading in it, as though he was desperate for company. While she knew she should leave, Hannah found herself rooted to the floor, curious to solve this mystery of a man.

"Tell me why you've escaped the festivities," he continued.

Hannah wandered over to the chesterfield now, where she would be closer to the enigma's corner of solitude.

"I don't particularly enjoy parties," she admitted, though why she was saying so to a stranger she couldn't even see, she wasn't sure. Perhaps it was because, with his visage obscured, he was unthreatening. "I find I can best get through them if I take a minute to myself now and again."

"I see," he said, and she felt that, more than simply offering platitudes, he actually did understand. "Are you certain you should be alone, unchaperoned?"

"Likely not," she said, looking down at her hands. "But my mother would not be particularly pleased to accompany me away from the party."

"You're to show yourself off – find a husband then?" His voice was deep and rough, as though it had been hindered by disuse.

"Something like that," she said softly.

"Well, you certainly won't find one in here," he said, a slight bit of rueful laughter accompanying his words, and Hannah wondered what it was about him that caused him to discount himself from fulfilling such a role.

"Are you married?" she asked, her curiosity getting the better of her.

"No."

"You have no wish to be?"

There was a long pause.

"No."

"Well," she said, needing to fill the silence suddenly, as the air that had previously carried some comfort in it suddenly became tense at his terse replies. "Not to worry. It seems I have already found myself one."

"Oh?"

"It's actually the purpose of this party tonight – to celebrate our betrothal. I don't know him particularly well. Our parents have arranged it all, you see. It's odd, isn't it? That I am to spend the rest of my life with someone I hardly know?"

He was silent for a moment once more, and Hannah longed to walk over and see what this man looked like. It was both disconcerting and yet at the same time freeing to speak to someone practically invisible.

"Are you sure he would make you a good husband?" the stranger finally asked, and Hannah sensed that there was more behind the words than a simple question.

"I don't know," she said, for he echoed the very sentiment she worried about. "It doesn't seem to matter."

"It should," he said, surprising her by standing. He walked around the perimeter of the room, never stepping into the dim glow from the fire. The room held no other source of light – the wall sconces, candles, or lanterns were all dark.

## THE CURSED PORTRAIT

"Do not give your life away to someone who doesn't deserve it."

Hannah stood, taking a few steps toward where he had paused in the corner of two bookshelves. He was tall, she could ascertain from his silhouette, his build lean and seemingly strong. His hair nearly brushed his shoulders, quite opposed to the style of the day. Her fingers itched to paint the scene before her.

"You seem to know more than you are saying," she said, knowing she should leave the room and not question her marriage, for it was too late. The betrothal had been announced, and there was no going back now. Her parents would never allow it. "Tell me what I should be aware of – please?"

He hesitated, and she could sense that he was trying to decide whether or not to share what she now so desperately needed to know.

"Your soon-to-be husband can be a brute, Lady Hannah," he said, and she gasped when he said her name, though why wouldn't he know who she was? He was at her betrothal party, after all, even if he was hiding away in the library. "He will not be true to you, will give you nothing but pain. Why do you think they are marrying him off to a woman like you? Should not a future earl be doing much better for himself? Your parents must be desperate."

Hannah could not have been more shocked had he slapped her in the face. She couldn't deny, however, that his words held truth to them, and caused the tingles of unease that had accompanied her the few times she had been with her betrothed to turn into full tremors.

"Pardon me, but who are you to say such things to me?" she finally managed, and his chuckle was low and humorless as he stepped forward, staying just beyond the soft light.

"I am a man who tells the truth, for I have no reason to

pretend, like the rest of them out there, cloaked in their fineries and their lies, obscuring their horrible souls beneath. With me, it is as you see it."

"And yet you hide in the shadows," she challenged, angry now that he would throw out such accusations without revealing anything about himself.

"You are correct," he acknowledged. "It is where I belong."

\* \* \*

EDMUND WONDERED why the girl was still here. He had to give her some credit – most young women would likely have gone running the moment they found themselves alone in the library with him. Although she hadn't yet actually *seen* him. The moment she did, he knew she would flee, as did everyone else with the unfortunate chance to see his visage. It was why he never should have come, why he belonged hidden away at the remote estate his father had been more than happy to give him, especially when he had promised to remain there.

Edmund would have preferred to not be here tonight, but his mother had insisted he attend. She felt the whole family should be supporting this marriage. Perhaps she knew they must do all within their power to force it ahead.

What was left of his heart went out to the girl before him. She was short and slim, with wide brown eyes and a waif-like quality about her. He had hoped that the woman his brother was to wed would be strong enough to hold her own against him. But this woman? She would likely break before him. He did admit, however, that she had some backbone, to remain here talking to a stranger in the darkness, especially after his insult.

He didn't overly care about the consequences that came

with warning her away from his brother and what awaited her were she to continue on with this marriage.

"It's not too late," he said, fighting the strange desire that coursed through him to step closer to her and touch the soft skin of her cheek where the firelight flickered. "You can go, still."

For a second, he wasn't sure if he was warning her away from him, or from his brother. Then he realized it didn't matter. It would be best for her if she ran away from his entire sordid family.

"I can't," she said, shaking her head with some melancholy. "It's been decided. My parents would never allow me to cry off now."

"Tell me," he said, the need to know coming from deep within him, "have you ever known a man before?"

"Have I ever... Oh! Of course not!" she exclaimed, her eyes widening as she peered at him, attempting to make him out in the darkness. "How could you ask such a thing?"

He shrugged, even though he knew she couldn't see him. "I was not trying to imply anything untoward. I was simply wondering if you have ever known any tenderness, so that you will have a fond memory to look back upon once your husband comes to you."

She audibly swallowed.

"No," she said, her voice just above a whisper. "I have never even been kissed."

He reached out, unsure what caused him to do so, and took her hands in his before gently pulling her toward him to join him in the shadows. He should now place his hands on her shoulders, turn her around, and steer her out the door. Away from him, from his darkness, from all the base instincts that drove him.

But he didn't. While his dark heart hadn't shown compassion to another person for years now, he felt an unnatural need to protect this woman, to provide her with all he knew his brother never would.

He didn't know why she went along willingly, unresisting. But comply she did, stepping forward, joining him in the darkness, tilting her head back to look up at him, and searching out his face.

Fortunately, however, the light was too dim and the fire too small for them to distinguish anything but silhouettes of one another.

It was enough for him to know where she stood, and he reached out slowly so as not to scare her, before he finally allowed his fingertips to graze the soft, smooth skin that had called to him since she had entered the room. He began to tilt his head down toward her, giving her every opportunity to back away, to run, to go tell all of the others about the monster in the library.

But she didn't. She stood there, expectant, head tilted back, the only sign of a change in emotions the increased speed of her breath, which puffed against his lips.

Until finally, his lips reached hers. He grazed them upon hers, softly tasting, testing, tempting her. When she stood on her tiptoes, placed her hands upon his chest, and leaned into it, he was lost.

He moved his lips over hers, still gentle, but now exploring, caressing, providing her with all of the care she deserved in a first kiss. He slid his hands down her face, her neck, her shoulders, until they wrapped around her back and pulled her against him.

She had been telling the truth of her inexperience, and yet it was her enthusiastic response that fueled him, driving him to delve deeper, to taste her sweet innocence. It flowed through him powerfully, reminding him that he was the last man who should be touching her. His brother might treat her ill, but at least she likely wouldn't be disgusted when she stared upon his face.

It was that thought that was finally strong enough to make him pull back, to leave the sweetness of her lips, though it was a moment before he could step away from her.

"There," he said gruffly, though inwardly he cursed, "remember that."

She stepped back from him, leaving him feeling bereft at the loss of her closeness. He didn't know how long they stood like that, staring at one another, suspended in indecision, until a shriek from beyond the room captured their attention.

"I must go," she said, and then, turning in a swirl of fabric and the scent of lavender, she was gone.

Keep reading Always Your Love!

## ALSO BY ELLIE ST. CLAIR

*Standalones*

The Cursed Portrait
Always Your Love
The Stormswept Stowaway
A Touch of Temptation

Regency Summer Nights Box Set
Regency Romance Series Starter Box Set

*Noble Pursuits*
Her Runaway Duke
Her Daring Earl
Her Honorable Viscount

*Reckless Rogues*
The Duke's Treasure (prequel)
The Earls's Secret
The Viscount's Code
The Scholar's Key
The Lord's Compass
The Heir's Fortune

*The Remingtons of the Regency*
The Mystery of the Debonair Duke
The Secret of the Dashing Detective
The Clue of the Brilliant Bastard

The Quest of the Reclusive Rogue

The Remingtons of the Regency Box Set

*The Unconventional Ladies*
Lady of Mystery
Lady of Fortune
Lady of Providence
Lady of Charade

The Unconventional Ladies Box Set

*To the Time of the Highlanders*
A Time to Wed
A Time to Love
A Time to Dream

*Thieves of Desire*
The Art of Stealing a Duke's Heart
A Jewel for the Taking
A Prize Worth Fighting For
Gambling for the Lost Lord's Love
Romance of a Robbery

Thieves of Desire Box Set

*The Bluestocking Scandals*
Designs on a Duke
Inventing the Viscount
Discovering the Baron
The Valet Experiment
Writing the Rake

Risking the Detective

A Noble Excavation

A Gentleman of Mystery

The Bluestocking Scandals Box Set: Books 1-4
The Bluestocking Scandals Box Set: Books 5-8

*Blooming Brides*
A Duke for Daisy
A Marquess for Marigold
An Earl for Iris
A Viscount for Violet

The Blooming Brides Box Set: Books 1-4

*Happily Ever After*
The Duke She Wished For
Someday Her Duke Will Come
Once Upon a Duke's Dream
He's a Duke, But I Love Him
Loved by the Viscount
Because the Earl Loved Me

Happily Ever After Box Set Books 1-3
Happily Ever After Box Set Books 4-6

*The Victorian Highlanders*
Duncan's Christmas - (prequel)

Callum's Vow

Finlay's Duty

Adam's Call

Roderick's Purpose

## Peggy's Love

## The Victorian Highlanders Box Set Books 1-5

*Searching Hearts*

Duke of Christmas (prequel)

Quest of Honor

Clue of Affection

Hearts of Trust

Hope of Romance

Promise of Redemption

Searching Hearts Box Set (Books 1-5)

*Christmas*

Christmastide with His Countess

Her Christmas Wish

Merry Misrule

A Match Made at Christmas

A Match Made in Winter

For a full list of all of Ellie's books, please see www.elliestclair.com/books.

## ABOUT THE AUTHOR

Ellie St. Clair is the creative mind behind Regency romances featuring strong, unconventional heroines and men who can't help but fall in love with them. Her novels perfectly blend passion, mystery, and suspense, transporting readers to a world where love conquers all, even the darkest secrets.

When she's not weaving tales of love and intrigue, Ellie can be found spending quality time with her husband, their children, and their beloved dog, Bear, a spirited husky cross. Despite her busy life, she still finds joy in the simple pleasures—whether it's savoring a scoop of her favorite ice cream, tending to her garden, or challenging herself in the gym. An avid plant enthusiast, she's on a never-ending quest to keep her indoor greenery thriving.

She also loves corresponding with readers, so be sure to contact her!

www.elliestclair.com
ellie@elliestclair.com

- facebook.com/elliestclairauthor
- x.com/ellie_stclair
- instagram.com/elliestclairauthor
- amazon.com/author/elliestclair
- goodreads.com/elliestclair
- bookbub.com/authors/elliest.clair
- pinterest.com/elliestclair

Printed in Great Britain
by Amazon